THE GRAY WHALES ARE MISSING

GULLIVER BOOKS
HARCOURT BRACE JOVANOVICH
San Diego   Austin   Orlando

THE GRAY WHALES ARE MISSING

ROBIN · A · THRUSH

Illustrated by DIANE deGROAT

Requests for permission to make copies of any part of the work should be mailed
to: Permissions, Harcourt Brace Jovanovich, Publishers, Orlando, Florida 32887.

Library of Congress Cataloging-in-Publication Data
Thrush, Robin.
The gray whales are missing / by Robin Thrush ;
illustrated by Diane de Groat.—1st ed.
p.   cm.
"Gulliver books."
Summary: Just as his matchmaking efforts seem to be working
with his widowered father and his favorite teacher,
ten-year-old Pence becomes involved in investigating
why the migrating gray whales have deviated
from their normal course off the California coast.
ISBN 0-15-200455-6
[1. Pacific gray whale—Fiction.   2. Whales—Fiction.
3. California—Fiction.   4. Teacher-student relationships—Fiction.
5. Single-parent family—Fiction.]   I. De Groat, Diane, ill.
II. Title.   PZ7.T418Gr 1987   [Fic]—dc19   87-17822 CIP AC

Printed in the United States of America

First edition

A B C D E

To my sons,
NICHOLAS *and* WILLIAM,
brave and Orthodox

To my father,
wise and unorthodox

CONTENTS

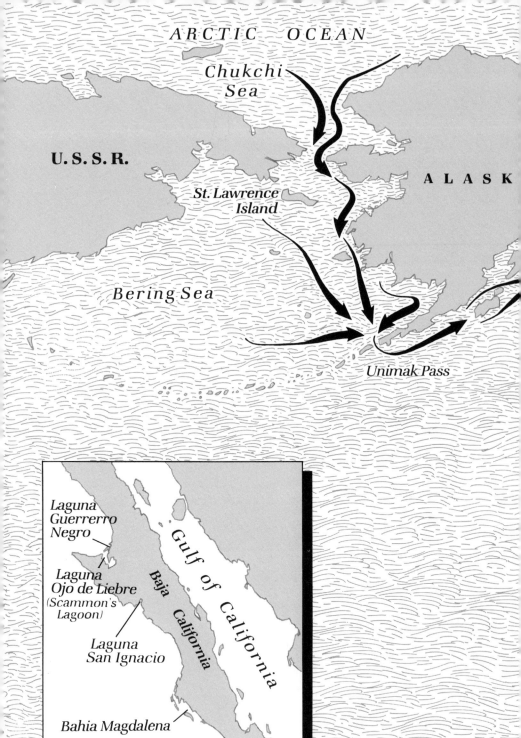

ARCTIC OCEAN

Chukchi
Sea

U.S.S.R.

St. Lawrence
Island

ALASK

Bering Sea

Unimak Pass

Laguna
Guerrero
Negro

Laguna
Ojo de Liebre
(Scammon's
Lagoon)

Laguna
San Ignacio

Bahia Magdalena

PACIFIC OCEAN

Gulf of California

Baja California

Cabo San Lucas

PACIFIC

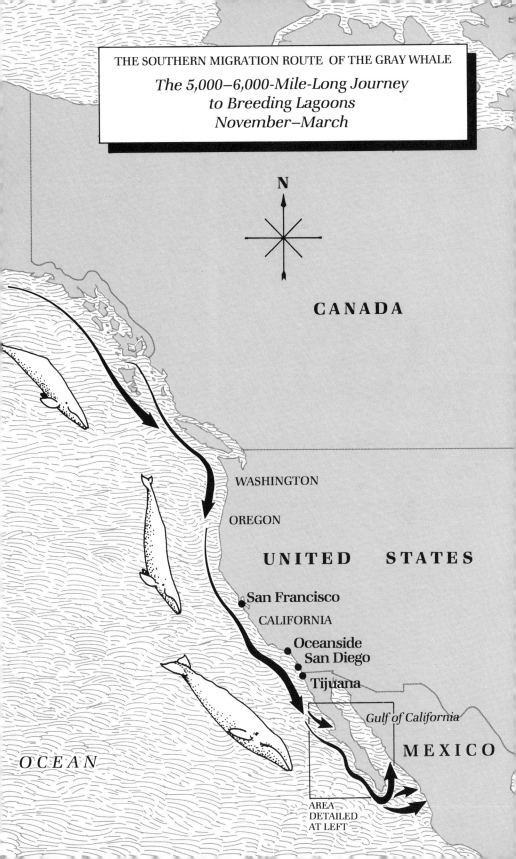

THE SOUTHERN MIGRATION ROUTE OF THE GRAY WHALE
*The 5,000–6,000-Mile-Long Journey
to Breeding Lagoons
November–March*

N

CANADA

WASHINGTON

OREGON

UNITED   STATES

San Francisco

CALIFORNIA

Oceanside
San Diego

Tijuana

Gulf of California

MEXICO

OCEAN

AREA
DETAILED
AT LEFT

THE GRAY WHALES ARE MISSING

1
QUESTIONS

Pence clung to the whale's back and took a deep breath. It dove down to the bottom of the pool in a matter of seconds and just as quickly broke through the surface of the water again and, with a powerful thrust of its flukes, leaped fifteen feet into the air. Pence held on, and felt like he was flying.

His father's voice, telling him to come down to breakfast, tugged him out of this dream he had had so many times before. What did it mean? Why did it keep coming back? Spenser "Pence" Thompson lay in bed a few more minutes, wondering if it would ever come true and why killer whales fascinated him so much. Maybe it was their unexpected gentleness, as much as their great power.

Pence's bed was pushed up next to the window. He opened the shutters and looked out toward Mission Bay. It was another glorious December day, too early for windsurfers and water-skiers, but

countless joggers were making their way around the curves of the bay. He knew the sand crabs were tucked safely underground until dark yet wondered if the pounding of human feet above frightened them. But do crabs hear? he asked himself.

Much to his father's dismay, Pence often did his homework sprawled on his bed. From there he had a good view of the bay and the way it reflected the night sky. He liked the sometimes fragrant, occasionally pungent smell of the water. He knew he never wanted to live anywhere else. For him, the center of the city wasn't downtown, it was right outside his window. For within Mission Bay Park lay Pence's second home, a huge marine zoological park called Sea World, where his father, Dr. Matthew Thompson, worked.

After the shroud of early-morning fog lifted, Pence could see the outlines of the park from his window. He did not actually need to see it, however. He kept a map of it tucked away in his mind. In fact, Pence was certain he could find his way around the park blindfolded, though he might need to take a peek when he got close to the open shark tank.

San Diego generally had fine weather, but Pence looked forward to occasional rainy or overcast weekends. The beaches were usually deserted then, and while other families shopped or lay in front of their televisions, Pence and his father took long walks, explored tide pools, or fished.

4

Enough daydreaming, he told himself. He stretched and walked to his closet, thinking of his friend Jonathan Glazer, who usually wore one of his many bright-colored Hawaiian shirt and Bermuda outfits and coordinated high-top sneakers. Jonathan's parents were divorced, and he seemed to have a lot of *things.* Pence wasn't sure he would look good in wild-colored clothes. He was too thin and, according to his father, all legs, like a colt. Jonathan was built like a tank.

Pence's father thought the only colors men and boys should wear were navy, gray, and khaki. "Fads never last long," he'd told Pence. But then, his father wasn't a true Californian. He had grown up in upstate New York and even after fifteen years of living in southern California, he did not understand how Pence could get so excited at the mere mention of convertible cars, skateboards, and jams—Bermuda-length bathing trunks that were the rage.

Pence put on his plain navy corduroy shorts and a navy-and-white-striped shirt. He brushed his wavy brown hair with the side of his hand, threw the comforter over his bed, and ran down the stairs two at a time.

His father was immersed in the morning paper, gripping it in one hand while he poured coffee with the other. He didn't seem to realize that he'd already overfilled the cup, and the brown liquid was running down the counter and onto his shoes.

"Dad!" shouted Pence, reaching for paper towels.

"First the earthquake, now an eruption of lava!" His father laughed as he surveyed the damage.

"What do you mean?"

"Didn't you feel the earthquake last night?"

Pence shook his head. It was the third earthquake he had slept or dreamt through in the last year. "Was it a big one?"

"No big damage reported, according to the radio news, but the tremors were recorded at 5.6 on the Richter scale. My bed moved this time," he said, raising his eyebrows.

Pence sighed. Nothing interesting like that ever seemed to wake him.

"You'll probably be more interested in this article on the baby whale," said his father.

"What does it say? There's nothing wrong, is there?" Pence asked anxiously.

"Now don't be such an alarmist," his father chided him. "Newspapers report *good* news as well as airline disasters, hurricane damage, and the rising crime rate!"

Pence looked over his father's shoulder and scanned the short feature on the baby killer whale. "The calf has passed the critical stage. . . . It has already gained 100 pounds since birth . . . very active . . . imitates its mother's behavior."

"I bet you know as much about whales as the reporter who wrote that story." His father smiled at him.

Pence blushed. "Only what you've taught me." He knew that killer whales have no natural enemies, hunt in groups, and can swim at amazing speeds. "I can't believe she's just a few weeks old."

His rumbling stomach prevented him from further thought on the subject. "Did you eat already?"

"No. I was waiting for you. But whatever it is, it better be quick. On second thought, maybe I'll grab something at work."

"My gym teacher says that's what's wrong with Americans," Pence said seriously. "We start our day off with sugar-coated doughnuts, white toast dripping with jam, or, even worse, food out of vending machines!"

"All those sound pretty good to me," his father replied.

"I'm offering something much better: bran cereal with fresh fruit."

"Didn't we have that yesterday?" asked his disappointed father.

"The day before," Pence corrected him, pouring the cereal into bowls, then adding sliced bananas and low-fat milk. He set a bowl in front of his father, who eyed it critically and returned to his reading.

Pence wondered how his father got to be head of penguin research at Sea World. He knew his father was quick-thinking and hard-working, and he had a real way with animals. But did he read all day long there, too?

To work successfully with animals, you need to be both calm and firm, even assertive. That's what Dr. David Blair, the park's head zoologist, had told Pence's fifth-grade class. When Pence had looked up "assertive" in the dictionary, one of the definitions given was "aggressive." Was his father aggressive? He didn't think so, and he wasn't sure that animal trainers or veterinarians should be too assertive. The next time he saw Dr. Blair, he hoped he could discuss this fine point. Maybe Dr. Blair would offer him a job.

"Whenever you feel you've had enough education, come and see me," Pence imagined Dr. Blair saying to him.

"I know my father would like me to finish elementary school," Pence would answer in his most mature manner.

Now, Pence looked across the table at his father, whom he judged to be both calm and firm, but also easily distracted. He seemed to be in another world when he had a newspaper or book in front of him.

"Do crabs hear, Dad?" he asked, breaking the silence.

His father looked perplexed. "Why do you want to know?"

Pence smiled at him. "You don't know, do you?" He was almost relieved on the few occasions when his father didn't have an immediate response.

"No. You caught me on this one," his father admitted. "But I hope they do."

"Me, too."

"I'll get the answer from someone at work."

"Sometimes," Pence said, "I think it's more interesting *not* to know the answer."

"Don't ever stop looking for answers, Pence," his father said thoughtfully.

As he got ready to leave, he said, "Come see me after school. I want to show you the new penguin chicks. There are gentoos, rockhoppers, macaronis—you name it."

Mr. Thompson walked out the back door to where their sabat was moored. The sabat was nothing more than a rowboat with a small sail attached, but it was the easiest way for him to get to work. If the wind was down, it was a ten-minute row across Mission Bay; with a good wind, it took only five minutes.

Pence, running the five long blocks to the school-bus stop, remembered he hadn't fed his fish and turtles. Well, he excused himself, it was hard enough to meet the bus at 7:40. This morning, he arrived just in time.

He climbed up the bus steps and looked down the aisle. Laura Kiefer was motioning that she had saved him a seat and before Pence had a chance to pull off his backpack and sit down, she was excitedly telling him that she'd overheard Miss Burdick talking to one of the sixth-grade teachers about their next field trip.

"It looks like we're going whale-watching next week. Isn't it a little early?" she asked.

Pence had no time to answer. She was already into her next question.

"Do you think the whales ever get tired of being followed and photographed by a lot of human beings in boats? By the way, what's the closest you've ever gotten to a whale?"

"Well, in my dream . . ." Pence wanted to say. He didn't know which question to answer first, but he knew from years of friendship with Laura that if he didn't speak soon, there would be even more questions. Their teacher, Miss Burdick, said Laura was destined to become a reporter.

Pence liked Laura a lot. She was good in sports and in school, and she didn't act silly, like most of the other girls he knew. But she did talk too much.

They sat together on the bus almost every day. Sometimes, Pence had to check his homework or wanted to look out the window and spot sports cars—one morning he had counted twenty-one Porsches on the way to school, and was trying to break that record—but Laura always had more questions.

Had his mother talked so much? Pence was sure she hadn't.

He told Laura that he didn't remember ever going whale-watching much before Christmas, but he knew that the scientists who studied and tracked whales went out anywhere from the first week in December to the first week in February.

"I did get very close to a killer whale once," he said, remembering the experience with a grin. "When I was about four, I was one of the people picked out of the audience at the killer whale show to be kissed by Shamu."

What he didn't tell Laura was how terrified he had been. He had clutched his mother's hand tightly when she walked with him to the enormous pool, assuring him the whole way that he wouldn't be the whale's lunch! What he would never forget was the whale's tongue—large and pink and warm against his small cheek.

"Now, I have a question for you," he said, pleased to be the interviewer, for a change. "When you're alone, Laura, do you ask *yourself* questions?"

Laura blushed. "I know I ask too many questions, but how else will I learn everything?"

"Speaking of knowing everything, are you ready for the spelling test?"

Laura nodded. She was a terrific speller.

"Well, can you quiz me?"

By the time they reached school, Pence had finally mastered "anxious" and "appropriate," but a few of the other ninety-eight "a" words on the test still escaped him. "Average," another "a" word, was all he would ever be in spelling, he concluded, silently.

2
SPECIAL ASSIGNMENT

As the bus turned into the school grounds, Pence stared out at the fifty-foot palm trees that formed a protective wall around the school. They reminded him, as they always had, of sentries on duty.

Jonathan Glazer swaggered over to meet Pence, giving him an appraising look.

"Who's your tailor, Spenser?" he remarked, shaking his head. He was the only one who ever called Pence by his given name.

"Very funny."

"Why don't you ask your father to give you a clothes allowance?" Jonathan's eyes were dancing. "Tell him you know how busy he is. Make him feel you're doing him a favor by removing this heavy burden," he urged.

Pence had to smile. Jonathan knew all the angles.

"Don't do Pence any favors," scoffed Laura, who was tagging along behind the boys.

"Listen, are you Spenser's guardian angel?" Jonathan glared at her. "And why are you always wearing your glasses on top of your head? One day they'll fall off, and you'll be blind as well as nosy!"

"Well at least I don't spend half my life in Mr. Moore's office!" she retaliated.

Jonathan drew an imaginary mark in the air with his right index finger. "Chalk one up for Miss Kiefer. Actually, I want you both to know I'm mending my ways. Look at my shirt! Don't I look prepared for the test?"

Jonathan's shirt was covered with writing. Pence was shocked. "You didn't really write the test words on your shirt, did you?"

"No," roared Jonathan. "But who knows? This shirt might be an inspiration to the class!"

Luckily for Jonathan, Miss Burdick found his shirt "amusing," and the morning passed smoothly. But at lunch, Jonathan started a food fight with a new boy named Manuel.

"I was just trying to find out if the kid was dumb! He never talks. I was conducting a scientific experiment!" Jonathan protested in vain. Miss Burdick pointed him in the direction of the principal's office.

Someone yelled after him, "You're the dumb one, Glazer." Laughter filled the lunchroom.

Pence got up from the table. Suddenly he had

no appetite for school food or the conversation of his peers.

Laura followed him out to the playground. "Why do you think he does it?" she asked earnestly.

"I don't know," Pence answered, shaking his head. "My dad says Jonathan is only trying to get attention, like a lot of kids whose parents are divorced."

"Well, I feel sorrier for someone like you," said Laura, without thinking. She gasped as Pence's face turned deep red. "Forgive me, Pence," she gulped, close to tears. "I shouldn't have said that. I'm sorry. Really."

"It's okay. . . . It's kind of funny the way every-one seems to go out of the way to avoid mention-ing my mom. She's been dead for more than two years."

Then, looking straight at Laura he added, "But you'll never be the great star reporter, Laura Kiefer, if you don't learn to keep some of your thoughts to yourself!"

She nodded. The school bell rang and they returned to their class in silence.

"Class, I have some good news for you," Miss Burdick announced. "We are going whale-watching next Friday."

A few of the worst students applauded. Pence caught Laura's eye and gave her the thumbs-up sign. She really *was* going to be a reporter, he thought.

"Since many of you have been whale-watching before, and undoubtedly will go again, I would like to make this year's trip a little more interesting for all of us."

She looked directly at Pence. "As our unofficial whale expert, Pence, I'd like you to prepare an oral report on gray whales." She paused. "By the way, does anyone know the scientific term for a whale expert?"

"Cetologist," Laura answered, before Pence had even had a chance to raise his hand.

"Correct. Pence, I would like you to deliver this report as we head out to sea. I hope your talk will help sharpen our powers of observation," she said encouragingly.

"All of you must bring a notebook and pencil with you that day," she emphasized. "You are to hand in a short essay on the gray whale and a sketch the following Monday.

"Pence, since I've asked you to prepare a talk, you're excused from the general assignment," she added.

"Talk about teacher's pet," complained a voice in the back.

"I don't know why someone is grumbling back

there," Miss Burdick said sternly, "but I will assign more work to anyone else who wants it." A rare silence filled the room.

"Well, if there are no questions, I see Mr. Arnold waiting outside. Your science class will be held outdoors today."

Laura jumped out of her seat and was the first one out the door. "Where are we headed, Mr. Arnold?" she asked eagerly.

"We're going to take advantage of this beautiful day to talk about the weather *outside* for a change— where weather belongs." He chuckled. None of the class thought it much of a joke.

Mr. Arnold cleared his throat and continued in a more serious tone. "Let's hike quickly over to the canyon. Before we get on with today's discussion I want to see if last night's earthquake tremors did any damage." He started to march off, but suddenly turned around and added, "In case I forget to tell you later, read chapter four in your text this weekend. You'll be quizzed on Monday."

Mr. Arnold reminded Pence more of an overgrown boy scout than a scientist. He wasn't at all like his father or Dr. Blair, who Pence knew were real experts. Mr. Arnold rubbed his hands together before beginning a lecture and often greeted the class with "Good afternoon, junior scientists." Then he'd talk for a half hour straight. Pence was convinced that Mr. Arnold got more out of his lectures than the class did.

Jonathan agreed with Pence and was fond of pointing out that "Mr. A." was the real junior scientist. Laura, on the other hand, used words like "gifted" and "genius" to describe their science teacher.

Pence caught up with Laura. "Why are you trying to earn Brownie points from Mr. Arnold?"

"Wait a minute," Laura said defensively. "What about the way you've been acting with Miss Burdick?" Without waiting for a response, she said slyly, "Mr. Arnold can't be all that bad. I saw Miss Burdick and him together at the Catch of the Day restaurant last weekend."

"That's im-impos-sible," Pence stammered. "The guy's pants are too short, and he's flatfooted, and he has that little mustache!"

"I never noticed he was flatfooted," Laura murmured. "Anyway, I think he's handsome. He's so tall. I bet he was a basketball star in college."

"Is there some problem?" interrupted Mr. Arnold, who often seemed to come out of nowhere.

"No. Laura and I were just discussing which city has the worst weather," said Pence, recovering quickly.

"And what did you decide?" asked Mr. Arnold, with genuine interest.

Pence smiled weakly and gave Laura an imploring look.

She took over easily. "Pence's father grew up in upstate New York and still talks about the severe winters there, so Pence picked Buffalo, New York. I said there were lots of other areas of the country besides the northeast with uncomfortable climates."

Laura was a born lecturer, maybe even a "junior politician," thought Pence. Mr. Arnold seemed spellbound.

"I picked Amarillo, Texas." She beamed. "It's unbearably hot in the summer and plagued by high winds in the winter."

"Good thinking, Laura," congratulated Mr. Arnold, shaking her hand excessively. "I'm encouraged to know that my students have serious discussions on their own."

Pence watched Mr. Arnold run up to some other junior scientists, probably to find out if they were talking about the weather, too.

He turned to Laura. "How do *you* know what the weather is like in Amarillo, Texas?"

"I've already finished chapter four," she said, looking smug.

While Mr. Arnold spoke about cloud formations and weather patterns, Pence tried to imagine Miss Burdick and Mr. Arnold together. Mr. Arnold probably chose a fish restaurant, he concluded, so she wouldn't notice that he reeked of formaldehyde. If Mr. Arnold wasn't lecturing, he was dissecting something in his lab.

Miss Burdick was pretty old, Pence guessed. Probably close to thirty. But she was tall and graceful. She wore her auburn hair tied up in a knot that always looked as if it was going to come undone. Pence sometimes found himself staring at her hands. They were beautiful. She used them when she talked, making the subject come to life. Even "C" students tried hard in her classes.

Pence elbowed Laura. "What is Arnold's first name anyway? He always signs his name D. W. Arnold, as if he's some important thinker."

"It's Delbert," Laura whispered. "But don't tell anyone. I think he's embarrassed about it."

Pence covered his mouth with both hands. What a name! Imagine giving someone a name like that, unless you knew he was going to grow up to be strange. But Old Delbert's parents had guessed right! He couldn't wait to tell Jonathan.

When he had fully recovered, Pence vowed to himself that, no matter what, he would never allow Miss Burdick to get serious about Delbert Arnold!

Walking home from the bus stop, the time of day he did his best thinking, Pence devised a strategy for stopping the enemy, in this case D. W. A., from overwhelming the ally, Miss Burdick. He named it Plan A–B. It wasn't an imaginative code name, but an easy one to remember, especially if he needed Laura's or Jonathan's assistance at any point.

Pleased with himself, Pence hummed a little tune. He paused in front of Pacifically Pets, a great store despite its name. The place was pretty busy for a weekday. A few of the kids inside were actually buying things. Pence decided to walk in, even though he only had twelve cents in his pocket, to inspect the new litter of puppies Laura had told him about. Once he found the four sleepy golden retriever pups, he couldn't take his eyes off them. The other kids seemed more interested in the hamsters, snakes, and exotic birds on display.

No unusual pets for me, Pence thought. He would gladly have taken the whole litter home. There was one huge obstacle, however: his father. To overcome that would take a more elaborate plan of attack. He considered Plan D (for dog and dad) as he dragged his backpack toward home.

3
TURTLE SOUP

When Pence reached home, he was greeted by the sound of the washer, dryer, and vacuum cleaner, humming in unison. He could also hear Carmen, their housekeeper, straining to reach the high notes of what sounded to him like a Mexican love song. He wasn't sure; Spanish was not his best subject.

"Can't a man occasionally come home to peace and quiet?" he shouted playfully. He hung his backpack on a hook in the front hall and headed for the kitchen.

The vacuum and the singing stopped, and Carmen came running, as Pence had hoped.

When she saw it was only Pence, and that he was all right, she put her hands on her hips, contorted her face, and said, "You know you supposed to *tell* me when you get home. You scare me half to death. I already have one big scare today."

Straightening up to her full five feet, two inches,

she added, "I only sing to keep fishes happy. I don't want them to die and then you blame me."

Carmen could be pretty dramatic, Pence thought. "Sorry. Anyway, I like your singing," he fibbed. "What scared you before?"

"The garage door move by itself *tres*—I mean three times," she whispered, looking around as she spoke.

"I'd better go check and see if anything is missing."

"I already do that. Everything is okay."

"Well, I'll tell Dad. Maybe there's something wrong with the electric motor." Then, to comfort her, he said, "I hope you weren't too scared."

"*Poquito.* A little," she admitted.

Carmen Martinez was the only grown-up Pence was allowed to call by her first name. She had worked for them on weekdays for as long as he could remember, and he was used to her way of speaking: leaving out words and mixing Spanish and English. He was always happy to find her there when he got home.

Every afternoon Carmen took the trolley back to Tijuana, a poor, crowded Mexican city just across the border. She shared a house with her sister, who took care of Carmen's three daughters in her absence. Pence felt he had something in common with Carmen. She had lost her husband in a car crash. He had lost his mother. He sensed that she felt the bond, too. She would do anything for Pence, and he knew it. Well, almost anything— she drew the line at feeding pets and cleaning their cages or tanks.

Pence opened the refrigerator half-heartedly. Its contents were as uninteresting as his clothes closet's. The cupboards were bare of snack foods, too. There were no bags of potato chips or chocolate-chip cookies or candy like at most of his friends' houses. When Carmen went grocery shopping, she really stuck to his list of healthy foods. Right then, though, he would have given a week's allowance for something soft and gooey, or crunchy and oily. Pushing aside boxes of cereal, rice, and spaghetti, he finally uncovered the honey-free, sugar-free granola bars that Jonathan had once refused as a snack, convinced that they would taste like sawdust. He thought it was "unnatural" for kids not to have a lot of sugar in their diet. Pence was beginning to agree, but rather than starve he grabbed two granola bars, sticking one in his pocket for later.

He had only himself to blame for the scarcity of junk food. The last time he saw his mother—in the hospital—she had made him promise to take good care of his father.

"You know your father," she'd said sweetly. "He'd forget to eat if someone wasn't there to remind him."

Pence had kept his promise. He was in charge of breakfast; Carmen prepared most of their dinners. They rarely had pizza, hot dogs, ice cream—or other normal American kid food—except for the times his father took him to a Padres game.

Thinking about food triggered another thought—he had forgotten to feed the fish and turtles that morning. He bounded up the stairs. Pence couldn't help wondering mischievously if Carmen's singing might one day be the death of them.

All seventeen fish were alive and swimming. They charged for the powdered food as he shook it generously over the tank.

Turning to Mortimer, one of his red-eared slider turtles, he remarked, "Don't you think they act like piranhas?" He patted Mortimer on his shell and asked where Max, his companion, was. A search failed to find him in or near the homemade habitat Pence and his father had fashioned for the turtles from a former hamster home. The turtles liked the tunnels and the maze as much as Herbert, the hamster, had.

When Herbert died of old age, he was barely three. At the time, Mr. Thompson had said that the next pet they got should have a longer life span and fewer teeth. Herbert, who managed to escape from every cage they built or bought, had chewed through wires and gnawed on chair legs when he had the chance.

What Pence really wanted was a dog. All his friends had dogs. Jonathan had two: a cock-a-poo at his mother's, a husky at his father's. Laura had named the cocker spaniel she got for her last birthday Eyewitness.

Pence's father felt it wasn't fair to get a dog and then leave it home alone all day. "It will bark and annoy the neighbors, like Sam's dog."

Sam Lewis lived two houses away. He was one of Pence's oldest friends, but because he went to private school, they didn't see much of one another, except on weekends and during vacations. Sam's dog, a terrier named Barney, was more than a year old, but he was no closer to being trained than he had been as a tiny pup.

Pence knew that his father's arguments were fair, but he also knew that if they had a dog, it would be a lot calmer and friendlier than Barney.

His fish, given to him by the curator of fishes, and his two "sort of rare" turtles had impressed his friends, however. Jonathan had taken pictures of the turtles, whom he had dubbed "the M and M Brothers." He'd also told Pence that he had the best "private" collection he'd ever seen. But you can't sleep with a fish or a turtle, or play catch, and they don't rush to greet you when you come home.

Carmen walked in to find Pence lying on his stomach, halfway under his bed, shining his flashlight here and there.

"What you doing now, Pence?" she asked sus-
piciously. "I clean there already."

"I'm looking for Max. He's missing again."

"Well, I very hungry today. I make delicious
soup," Carmen teased.

"Very funny," said Pence, getting up. "But I'm
supposed to meet Dad at work, and I can't leave
until I make sure Max is safe."

A few minutes later, Carmen called from the
bathroom that the animal was taking a shower and
she was leaving.

Pence yelled to her to wait for him. He carried
the wandering reptile back to Turtle Park, where
Mortimer was waiting by their plastic pool and palm
tree.

"Now stay, or I'll let Carmen make soup out of
you!"

Carmen was waiting by the back door.

"I hate to ask another favor, Carmen. I know how
much you do for us already," he said sincerely, "but
I want to invite my teacher over for dinner. I'd like
it to be a really special meal."

"Your father know this teacher?" Carmen asked.

Pence hesitated. "Well, kind of."

Carmen laughed. She had a big, hearty laugh
for such a small woman.

"I mean, I know Dad would really like her if he
knew her better. But I'll have to make the arrange-
ments. My father is *so* busy."

"I understand. You just tell Carmen when, and I make great Mexican dinner."

Pence threw his arms around her.

"You're terrific!"

He hopped on his bike and, as he raced off, he could still hear Carmen's laughter. It seemed to propel him forward. He should be at Sea World in fewer than fifteen minutes.

4
ALL KINDS
OF TROUBLE

By the time Pence arrived at the park, the last shows had ended. Only a few visitors remained, most of whom were taking photographs or buying souvenirs. At this time of the day, it seemed to Pence that the park was almost all his to explore and enjoy. He sometimes wished there were whole days when it was closed to the public.

His father's office was in a small blue building behind the penguin exhibit, far from the main entrance. Pence liked the long walk, because he passed the killer whale pools on the way. Checking his watch, he decided he had time for two quick detours. He stopped first to check on the seals and sea lions. When he unwrapped the granola bar he'd brought from home, one of the sea lions barked hopefully.

"Sorry, pal. This is *my* snack. Anyway, you look like you were well-fed today." As he rounded the corner of the killer whale pool, he could still hear the sea lion's baleful bark.

Bill McCormick, the head trainer, was there writing in a large notebook. It was the first time Pence had ever seen him wearing street clothes. Usually, he was in a wetsuit. Pence thought he looked uncomfortable.

"Nice to see you, Pence. I can guess why you're here." Mr. McCormick gave him a big smile.

"Well, actually, I came to see the new penguin chicks, but I thought I'd check on baby Shamu first."

"She's three weeks old today. I was just updating her growth and feeding charts."

"My dad showed me the article on her in this morning's paper," Pence said. "It sounds like you've taught her a lot already."

"She's learned twenty new behaviors this week alone," Mr. McCormick said proudly.

Pence wanted to ask what some of them were— he knew Laura would—but he had another thought. "Could you use some of your training methods on other animals? Dogs, for instance?"

"I do all the time," he answered matter-of-factly.

"Well . . . I have this friend who has this crazy terrier. He could really use some of your advice."

It turned out that Mr. McCormick had two dogs, which he'd taught to stay on unfenced property, among other achievements. Pence scribbled a few of his suggestions on the back of his homework.

"Let me know how your friend progresses. And remember to tell him it takes patience!" Mr. Mc-Cormick exclaimed.

Pence could hear and smell the penguin lab long before he reached it. He opened the heavy door and was surprised to find his father standing next to the counter holding syringes filled with food out to two hungry chicks. Many others, huddled in portable incubators, peeped impatiently.

"I'm sure glad to see you," he said wearily. "I can really use an extra hand for a few minutes. Make up some of our special formula, will you? These chicks are ravenous."

"Penguin milk shake coming up! Where *is* everybody?"

"Three people are out with the flu. Joe is making ice for the exhibit. Kate is ministering to some penguins in intensive care. Roberto is feeding the adults. I sent Hank up to the Los Angeles Zoo today. I guess the rest of my staff have gone home."

Pence set to work. He opened one of the refrigerators and took out the necessary ingredients: heavy cream, herring fillets, krill, and multivitamins. He carefully poured the correct amounts of each into a blender, turned it on, and watched the mixture thicken. It didn't look like a very appetizing concoction, but the penguins seemed to love it.

"Fill up enough syringes to satisfy these chicks, weigh the ones I've fed, and you can take your tired dad home."

Pence knew his father's system well. He checked each chick's tag number, weighed it, and recorded its weight in a box on the growth chart. He understood why the chicks needed tags: members of the same species all looked alike. He had asked his father once how aviculturists, bird keepers, told the males from the females. His father had joked that it wasn't easy, but as long as the penguins themselves knew, that was what really mattered.

"I've got something to tell you, Pence," his father said slowly, a little later. "It's about my work here. I've been doing too much of my research sitting at a computer since your mother died. I'm going to have to start making field trips again. We have about 500 penguins here, but we need a lot more if we hope to open our Texas park exhibit on schedule next year."

"Is that all you wanted to tell me?" asked Pence, who had thought the news was going to be much worse.

"That's part of it. Do you understand what it means, though?" his father pressed him.

"You won't be home as much. Right?"

"Right."

"And I'll have to stay with another family while

you're away." Pence gulped. "Well, I guess that's part of being a penguin expert," he added, hoping he sounded grown up. "Do you have to leave for somewhere soon?"

"I was coming to that part." His father hesitated. "I have to go to the Antarctic. Ideally, I should be there this minute—or better yet, last week— collecting the eggs before they hatch. It's much more difficult to transport live chicks."

"You won't be gone for Christmas, will you?" Pence asked anxiously.

"I'm afraid so," sighed his father. "We're dependent on the Chilean Air Force, and they can only fly us there later this month. We leave two days before Christmas and will be back in mid-January."

Pence was afraid if he spoke he'd burst into tears, so he waited for his father to say something more.

"Dr. Blair said he'd understand if I didn't make the trip . . . but I had no choice, son." He swallowed hard. "You know that I don't want to spend Christmas without you, but I can't change the penguins' breeding schedule."

Pence attempted a smile.

"Since we've spent the last few holidays with the Lewises, I figured you'd probably want to stay with them," his father continued. "If not, Uncle Buzz and Aunt Nan would love to have you stay with them in Syracuse. You might enjoy seeing snow for a change."

Pence didn't respond right away. He was working out a new plan. "Couldn't we hire someone to stay with me? Lots of kids have live-in housekeepers because their parents work."

"If that's what you really want, I'll ask Carmen if she knows anyone," his father said reflectively.

Suddenly, Pence's face brightened as the plan took on another shape. "What about Miss Burdick?" he almost shouted.

"You mean your teacher?" asked his incredulous father. "What made you think of her?"

"She's a really great person, Dad, and she lives alone in an apartment. It's probably small and dark and . . ."

"Pence, really," his father interrupted him.

"All right. But she told me she planned to come to Mission Bay as much as possible over the vacation!" he said triumphantly, feeling the way he imagined a detective would having just solved a difficult case.

"Not so fast, Pence. How do you know she doesn't have other plans for Christmas? If she's like most teachers, she probably wants to spend her free time as far away as possible from kids."

Pence wasn't going to be discouraged. "She likes me, Dad. I think we should invite her over for dinner, and then you'll see I'm right."

There, he'd said it. It wasn't as hard as he'd thought it would be. Of course, when your father tells you he's leaving you alone on Christmas, he'll probably agree to anything.

"Well, all right. But I hope you don't have any ulterior motive."

"Like what?" Pence tried to sound nonchalant.

"Apple polishing."

"How could you think that?" Pence demanded. He'd gotten almost all A's on his last report card. But when his father eyed him quizzically, he quickly said, "Well, maybe, a little."

As they went on with their work, Pence was thinking about Miss Burdick and how he had accomplished the first step in Plan A–B.

"Did I tell you," his father asked, "that killer whales, giant pandas, and penguins have become three of the most popular attractions at zoos and marine parks? Dalmations are becoming a popular dog breed again, too. There's been an increased attraction to black-and-white animals."

Pence's ears had perked up at the word "dog," but he decided not to pursue that now. "We're probably not likely to get a lot more interested in skunks, though," he noted instead.

Watching his father feeding a chick, Pence asked, "Why did *you* get interested in penguins, Dad?"

"On days like today, I'm not sure," his father confessed. "I think I was getting bored with other birds."

"All 12,000 kinds of them?" Pence asked.

"The number of species is closer to 8,000," his father corrected him gently. "But yes. Penguins were an unknown. They lived far away. I wanted to help determine if any of the seventeen species were endangered."

Pence was growing restless and hungry. "Why haven't you finished feeding that last chick?"

"I tried to give him an ounce of milk shake just before you arrived, but he ate so little I thought I'd try again before we left."

It was the smallest emperor chick Pence had ever seen. "Is it going to live?" he asked.

"I think its chances will be better if I keep a close eye on it."

Pence watched, mystified, as his father lined a Styrofoam ice chest with towels.

"What are you doing, Dad?"

"Adding a little excitement to our weekend," his father answered. "Luckily, I left the van here yesterday. We're taking this chick home. It's seriously underweight and dehydrated."

Pence looked somewhat disappointed.

"Don't worry," his father added. "We'll fit some fun in around the chick's schedule."

"What do you mean by 'fun'?" Pence asked warily.

"You didn't seriously think I'd leave you alone

at Christmas and not try to make up for it some-how, did you?" His father's face lit up.

Pence's mind raced. Was his father going to get him that ten-speed bike he'd been asking for? An expensive wetsuit, like the one Sam had? Were they going on that fishing trip his father had promised him last summer? Was it possible his father had seen the puppies at Pacifically Pets and changed his mind about getting a dog?

"Give me a hint," he pleaded.

"Not a chance," said his father, shaking his head. "I'm going out to warm up the van. I'll be back for you two in a few minutes."

As soon as the door closed, Pence grabbed the phone and made several important calls: first, to get Miss Burdick's number, who, when he called, was home and said she'd "love to come to dinner next Friday"; second, to Laura.

"How about some chick-sitting this weekend?" he asked.

"Pence, are you speaking in some sort of code?" For once, Laura was completely baffled.

"No. My dad's bringing home a sickly penguin chick. I thought you'd like to come over and see it and maybe help feed it."

"Sounds great. I'll come prepared," she promised.

Pence didn't dare ask for an explanation. Know-ing Laura, it meant a notebook and pencil, at least, and probably an "article" later. She always seemed to be working away enthusiastically. You couldn't help but admire her eagerness.

"Listen," Pence continued, "I've got something to talk to you about. It's important, but I've got to go now," he said, losing his courage. He hung up before she could start her questions and quickly called Jonathan, then Sam, and invited them over to see the chick the following morning.

On the way home, Pence felt almost faint and slightly nauseated. The night air was warm enough, but the heater was turned on full blast, to keep their precious cargo comfortable. On top of that, the chick gave off a peculiar odor, like meat starting to go rancid.

"What should we call the chick?" his father asked cheerily, oblivious to the heat and the smell. "How about Pompey, after the great Roman general? Or Peregrine, in honor of the falcon?"

"Really, Dad."

"Would you prefer Porky? Well, Popeye then? I've got it! Pee Wee, after that character you watch on TV."

"Stop!" Pence laughingly protested. He loved his father's word games, but he already had a name picked out.

"Let's call him Trouble. I can see that's what he's going to be."

Overcome by the day's events Pence went directly to bed after supper. His dreams were full of apprehension. When he reached out to grab hold of the whale, the giant creature swam away from him. Then it disappeared.

5
QUARANTINE CONDITIONS

"Keep your eye on Trouble, Pence. I'm going running," his father called up the stairs.

Pence closed the heavy textbook he'd been half reading in bed. How was he supposed to study for the big science test, write a report on the gray whale, help out with a pint-sized penguin chick, *and* have fun?

"Weekends aren't all they're cracked up to be!" he shouted, startling the fish.

A little while later, the doorbell rang. Trouble's first visitors had arrived. Sam had his football and Daisy, his sister, was carrying a stuffed penguin.

"Where's the new member of the family? I want to show him a few pattern plays," Sam said grinning.

"I brought my penguin to keep Trouble company," Daisy offered.

Sam rolled his eyes. Pence didn't understand

why Sam always acted as if Daisy were an alien or not his real sister. Pence was sure that having a younger sister was better than being an only child. In any event, he guessed the toy would prove a better companion for the chick than the football. He led them toward the family room.

"Be prepared! My dad has turned the heat up to what he calls 'brooding temperature.' Also, no one is allowed to touch the chick until you've passed Dad's inspection. We're operating under quarantine conditions," he explained, mimicking his father.

Both Sam and Daisy were surprised at how small and downy Trouble was. Daisy carefully placed her stuffed penguin in the makeshift incubator, but the chick didn't seem to notice.

"Listen, my dad wanted me to ask you and your dad to come along on our boat today. We're leaving around noon," said Sam.

"Great!" Pence exclaimed. Then his face fell. "What about the penguin?"

"We can take him with us," Sam suggested hopefully. "He's got to learn about the sea *someday!*"

"He's a born surfer," Pence joked, just as his father walked through the door.

"Talking about me, son?" his father asked with a grin, then greeted Daisy and Sam warmly.

A short time later, he motioned to the children, who were about to head outdoors, and they all watched in wonder as Trouble inspected the toy. He peeped at it, then nestled against it and fell asleep.

When Sam mentioned the boat trip, Mr. Thompson asked if they could have a rain check. "I've planned something special with Pence for the rest of the weekend."

Sam shot Pence a quizzical look. Pence shrugged his shoulders in response.

"Who will look after Trouble?" Pence asked.

"I called Hank. He's coming to pick him up shortly."

The doorbell rang again. Laura struggled in, loaded down with books.

"Sorry, I'm late," she said breathlessly, "but I stopped at the library first. I checked out a few books on penguins and two on child care. We've got to make sure the chick is happy as well as nourished. A positive attitude is important to the chick's chances of survival at this critical stage. Now where is the patient?"

Sam and Daisy were speechless. Laura had that effect on a lot of people, even some grown-ups.

After a few minutes of discussion, mostly between Laura and his father, Pence and Sam left Daisy and Laura to chick-sit while they went off on another important mission: a behavior training session with Barney, the terrier.

"What do you think your dad's planning?" Sam asked as they walked to his house, tossing the football on the way.

"I don't know," Pence offered lamely. "Dad's not giving any hints."

"But Christmas is only a few weeks away," Sam reminded him.

Pence wasn't in the mood to discuss Christmas. He knew the Lewises would offer to have him stay with them and he considered them the next best thing to family. But he didn't want them thinking he was their adopted son. He did have a father and his own home.

Barney greeted Pence affectionately, but was soon barking wildly, for no apparent reason.

"You can see he's still a long way from being trained," Sam admitted.

"Quiet, boy. There's hope for you yet." Pence turned to Sam. "Mr. McCormick gave me some pointers. First of all, punishments—like spanking or shoving Barney in the garage—will only make the problem worse. Punishment is a kind of attention.

"According to Mr. McCormick," Pence continued, "the first step in training any animal, once you and the animal are friends, is to reward good behavior and not overreact to bad. I took some notes," Pence said, pulling from his pocket a crumpled piece of paper that was once his homework. Smoothing it out, he read, "Consistency leads to boredom, which leads to frustration and aggression."

"Makes sense," replied Sam, "but what do I do about it?"

"You change the rewards, and the order in which you play with him and teach him. Mr. McCormick told me that he and his staff use a computer to keep track of their sessions with the whales and dolphins."

After an hour of trying to apply Mr. Mc-Cormick's suggestions, Pence and Sam were both worn out. Yet Barney seemed eager for more.

"I guess we made some progress," said Pence, half-heartedly.

"Maybe we should hire Mr. McCormick to train Barney," Sam suggested brightly.

The boys headed back to Pence's house. A white limousine was parked there; the chauffeur sat inside listening to a football game.

Slapping himself on the forehead, Pence said, "I forgot about Jonathan."

They arrived in time to hear Jonathan, who was decked out in a white linen suit, explain that he was going out to lunch with his father and some "woman he seems to be bonkers over."

"Do you think it's serious?" Laura asked him.

"Well, I'm not sure. But I bet my mom hopes it's not," he added softly.

Uncomfortable with the direction the conversation was taking, Pence pulled him toward the chick.

"Not so fast, Spenser. I promised my father I wouldn't get too close to the little creature, because of my new clothes, which, you may have noticed, make me a natural for a penguin look-alike contest."

Pence had to agree. "Black hair, white suit, torpedo-shaped body. Yes, you meet all the requirements." He laughed.

Holding in his stomach, Jonathan admitted he'd been overindulging on candy canes of late, trying to get in the Christmas spirit.

"You'll notice I brought along my trusted camera. Few people have the opportunity to have exotic flightless birds in their home," he said, "so I hope you'll allow me to record this momentous event."

After much wild posing and joking, Jonathan said his "carriage was waiting" and left. Minutes later, Mrs. Lewis arrived to collect Sam and Daisy.

"What was the important thing you wanted to talk to me about?" Laura asked immediately.

Pence didn't seem to hear the question.

"Can you believe Mr. Glazer may be getting

married again? That means Jonathan will have two mothers and I . . ." Pence stopped himself in mid-sentence.

"Pence Thompson, you know as well as I do that Jonathan wants nothing more than to have his parents back together."

He nodded glumly. "I don't know what's the matter with me lately."

"Maybe you're one of those people who gets depressed at holidays," she offered. "Or maybe you just realized you didn't ask for anything really great for Christmas."

"The things I want aren't possible," he answered flatly. Pence didn't need to explain to Laura what the most important "thing" was.

"Do you want to talk about it?" she asked gingerly.

Pence swallowed a few times before telling her about his father's trip to the Antarctic, and having to be alone at Christmas. When he had finished, Laura was close to tears, but she knew that if she started crying, Pence would too, or, worse, he would try to console her. She knew she had to be a good listener for a change.

They cheered up somewhat when he got to the part about asking Miss Burdick to dinner. "I'm worried about it," he confessed. "Do you think you could come over, too?"

"I'm sure I can." She grinned, relieved to be of some help. "But you'd better tell your dad and Miss Burdick that you've invited me. In my experience, grown-ups don't seem to like surprises."

"I guess you're right. Thanks for everything." Pence managed a smile.

"One question, only one," Laura promised. "Did you invite Miss Burdick over because of what I told you about her and Mr. Arnold?"

"Well, let's say it got me going!"

6
MISSING!

If it had not been for the overnight fishing trip his father had surprised him with right after Trouble's departure, it would have been one of the worst weeks of his life, Pence decided. School had been one test and one paper after another. The more he studied, the less he seemed to retain. His mind wandered uncontrollably to past Christmases, and to the one looming ahead, which he wished had already come and gone.

There was only one puppy left at Pacifically Pets, and it didn't look as if he was going to get it, despite all the hints he'd dropped and notes he'd posted on the refrigerator and slipped into his father's briefcase. His father was too busy preparing for his trip and trying to find someone to stay with Pence.

Pence had prayed that he would come down with laryngitis, or some other non-life-threatening illness, so he'd be excused from giving the whale talk. But three hours before they were to leave he still showed no signs of oncoming infirmity. He felt his forehead. It was cool as a whale's skin. He examined his tongue in front of the bathroom mirror. It wasn't nearly as large as Shamu's, but it was almost as pink.

Then he quickly scolded himself. What *was* he thinking of? He couldn't get sick. Miss Burdick was coming to dinner that night. And his father, who had given him some great ideas when they were out fishing, liked his whale report.

As he cleaned his room, gathering crumpled papers, textbooks, and the remains of the previous night's "brain snack," Pence remembered what Laura had told him during one of their lengthy phone conversations that week. "Teachers love to see where and how their students live. They especially like it when you show them your room and all your favorite things in it."

Pence wasn't exactly sure why he believed everything Laura told him. He had no idea where she even got most of her information. However, when it came to important things or people he cared about, he usually followed Laura's advice, and he was taking no chances with Miss Burdick.

After breakfast, Pence reminded his father not to be late coming home and boldly suggested that he change into something "that isn't plain gray."

"But isn't this Gray Whale Day?" his father joked.

Pence just shook his head, trying not to laugh.

At the bus stop, Laura asked Pence how long he thought his talk would run. Patting his backpack, Pence suddenly realized that his report was still lying on his bed, along with two about-to-be-overdue library books.

"Here, take this," he said, hurling his backpack at Laura. "Try to get the bus driver to wait."

Pence raced back home, grabbed the report and the books, stopping only long enough to catch his breath, and was back at the bus stop in what must have been record time. But the bus had come and gone.

Kicking at a stone in frustration, Pence shouted to the sky, "THIS IS NOT STARTING OUT TO BE A VERY GOOD DAY. PLEASE TRY A LITTLE HARDER TO MAKE THE REST OF IT BETTER!"

At home, he telephoned the school secretary to say he'd missed the bus and asked her to tell Miss Burdick that he'd meet the class at the landing.

With almost an hour and a half to kill, he walked around the house, checking for things that might be potentially embarrassing or just plain ugly. He carried stacks of his father's reading material out to the garage and removed two prominently displayed photographs: himself as a baby, and his parents. He worked quickly, hoping to have enough time to stop at the pet shop.

Giving the room one last look, he remembered that his mother had always had several vases filled with flowers. He hastily wrote a note to Carmen asking her to buy some.

At Seaforth Landing, he had no difficulty locating the *China Seas*, the fishing boat they were scheduled to go on.

While he waited for his class, he flipped through his whale report and began reading aloud. " 'Baleen whales are plankton eaters. . . .' What am I doing? That's page two." The seagulls made a perfect audience. They didn't criticize when he tried out several tones of voice and different stances. He tried to make points with his hands, the way Miss Burdick did. She was better at it, he decided, so he'd try to keep one hand at his side.

When the bus pulled up, Jonathan rushed over to ask Pence if he'd missed the bus intentionally. Pence didn't respond; his attention was focused on a figure stepping off the bus dressed in white pants and brand-new boat shoes, with a boatswain's whistle around his neck. It was none other than Delbert Arnold.

Laura was more interested in a stranger boarding their boat. She detected something odd about him. After all, why would a person go out whale-

watching dressed in a suit and carrying a brief-case?

"It hadn't occurred to me that old Delbert would be coming with us," Pence remarked.

"You can be sure *I* didn't invite him!" Jonathan vowed. Turning to Laura, he added, "Perhaps Miss Kiefer is to blame."

"Listen, you two," she rejoined, "Mr. Arnold has to be here. As far as I know, this field trip comes under the heading of science."

"Don't be too sure until *after* you've heard Spenser's talk!" Jonathan added.

Applying suntan cream to his pale face and arms, Mr. Arnold said, "It's a good idea to defend yourself against the sun's powerful rays." He then donned a navy-and-white captain's cap.

"What do you say we tie Arnold up and lock him below deck for the rest of the trip?" Pence suggested to Jonathan.

"Why bother? Let's just feed him to the sharks," Jonathan brashly suggested.

Over the loudspeaker, Captain Sweeney informed them of the safety rules they should all follow while aboard, the length of their trip, and the kinds of marine life they were likely to see.

Hoping to learn more about the stranger on board, Laura headed for the control room. No one noticed her slip away. She arrived just in time to overhear Captain Sweeney say to one of the mates, "These kids could be disappointed today."

"What are we going to tell that reporter?" the mate asked.

So that's who the stranger is! Laura thought. She would never have guessed. She wanted to pass on what she'd heard to Pence, but Mr. Arnold blew his whistle and asked everyone to be quiet.

"The next time I blow this whistle, I hope it's because I've spotted a whale, and *not* because one of you is misbehaving," he admonished. "Now, Pence, inspire us with your insights into these mighty beasts."

Pence caught Miss Burdick's eye. She smiled back at him. He began, somewhat nervously. " 'Once an endangered species, the California gray whale has made a miraculous comeback. Nowadays, close to 16,000 of them make the 6,000-mile journey along the Pacific coast between their summer home in the Bering Sea to their winter breeding grounds in the lagoons of Baja California. Theirs is the longest migration of any animal, and one of the most closely watched. . . .' " He went on to present what he thought were interesting facts about gray whales: that some scientists believe they don't eat anything during their migration; that the breeding ritual involves two males and one female. . . .

Before he'd finished, a number of his classmates were hanging over the side of the boat, each trying to be the first to sight a whale. Jonathan was taking photographs of everything, from Mr. Arnold's new shoes to the pelicans perched on buoys. At least he seemed to be listening, Pence thought. But where was Laura? His eyes searched the deck.

His gaze rested on Mr. Arnold who, like a killer whale, circled closer toward his unsuspecting prey—Miss Burdick—until he was inches away.

That action ruffled Pence so much he forgot where he was in his talk. He decided to end it early.

"My father, who's an aviculturist—he studies birds—believes that people have come to love and respect animals by seeing them up close, even touching them," he said.

A classmate asked, "So why does Jacques Cousteau believe that keeping any wild animals in captivity is wrong?"

Mr. Arnold's ears seemed to perk up at the mention of the famous oceanographer. He moved a few steps away from Miss Burdick and fixed his eyes on Pence.

Pence wished he knew the "right" answer to that question. Maybe there wasn't one.

"I've spent a lot of time around killer whales, watching them in training mostly," he answered. "I've seen them respond to humans they trust. I know that many of them have lived longer in captivity than they would have in the wild." He paused. Borrowing from beliefs his father expressed often, he added, "If there were no zoos, no Sea Worlds, no wildlife preserves, we'd never know what some animals are like." He stopped there and went to look for Laura.

He found her, as usual, with her little red notebook in hand.

"I think I've got our first clue," she said, matter-of-factly.

"What do you mean 'clue'? Where have you been?"

"I overheard the captain talking with Tom when we first came on board. They seemed to be worried about not seeing the whales this far south yet."

"Wait a minute," he interrupted. "Who is Tom?"

"He's that tall, blond boy," she answered, pointing to a member of the crew. "He works for Captain Sweeney over vacations. He's home from college for Christmas break."

"I'd just as soon hear about the whales," Pence muttered.

"Okay. Here are my facts," she said in her reporter voice. "The captain didn't seem approachable, but Tom volunteered—after I pestered him—some interesting information. It seems a pod of whales was sighted up the coast a few days ago, but it's vanished!"

Pence couldn't believe his ears. While he'd been wading through his report, Laura had been off investigating, possibly uncovering, a mystery— maybe even a disaster.

"Should we say something to Miss Burdick?" he asked, feeling confused.

"I don't know, Pence. I promised Tom I wouldn't breathe a word of what he told me," she confessed.

Pence shook his head. "Just promise me you won't go into the spy business," he teased. "Let's go and talk this over with Jonathan."

"Oh, there's one more thing." Laura stopped him. "A reporter from the *Sentinel* is on board."

Pence looked all around him. He hadn't seen anyone else on the boat.

Laura went on: "The crazy thing is he's not their science reporter. He told me he's here to write their usual once-a-year piece on whale-watching."

Pence looked at his watch. "It's certainly time we saw some whales," he said thoughtfully.

Minutes passed, then half-hours. But after two hours, they had yet to see a single fluke, much less the family pods they had expected.

Jonathan noticed Mr. Arnold climbing the steps to the bridge. He poked Pence. "Where do you think Mr. A. is headed?"

"I don't know, but I'm not going to wait around to find out," Pence replied. Laura and Jonathan were right behind him as he, too, went up to the bridge.

"I've made two trips a day all week and haven't sighted a whale yet," they heard Captain Sweeney say.

"What about north of here?" Mr. Arnold asked.

Rubbing his chin, the captain answered, "Aye, a large group was seen about 150 miles north a few days ago, but they've—" he hesitated—"disappeared." He waved a finger at Mr. Arnold and said warningly, "We don't want this to get out, now, do we? There may be nothing wrong." He had to protect his livelihood.

Mr. Arnold addressed the class back on the main deck. "Let's see, gray whales travel an average of 8.5 kilometers per hour. That's about five miles an hour." Turning to Pence, he asked, "Didn't you state in your report that they travel as much as 100 miles a day?"

"Yes, sir," Pence answered quickly.

"Well then, some of them should be here by now," Miss Burdick observed.

"Why hasn't there been anything in the news?" Laura wondered aloud, making sure the reporter, who was lingering nearby, heard her. He flicked the cigarette he'd just lit overboard, and walked off.

"Maybe they're not late," Jonathan suggested excitedly. "Maybe they're . . ."

"MISSING!" they all shouted at once.

"Don't jump to conclusions," Mr. Arnold interjected calmly. "Remember, the captain said it's still early."

He pressed on: "Does anyone have any thoughts on why the whales are late?"

Jonathan was the first to raise his hand. "My guess is they were tired of making the same old trip year after year and have joined the humpback whales in Hawaii, where the living is easier."

"They lost their passports!" shouted someone.

"Do you think Thompson's talk scared them away?" one boy asked mischievously.

While most of the class hooted, Manuel quietly ventured a comment. "My father told me they're drilling for oil in the Baja lagoons. Maybe the whales were bothered by it and have moved to new breeding grounds."

Miss Burdick smiled at him and thanked him for offering the "first sensible explanation."

"Let's hear some other *intelligent* suggestions," Mr. Arnold coaxed them.

That got their minds racing, and more thoughtful comments came quickly.

Laura speculated that the food supply may have lasted longer than usual in the Bering Sea. "Maybe that threw the whales off schedule. Maybe those whales that were sighted north of here are lingering. Pence said that wasn't uncommon."

"What about an oil spill?"

"Pollution," volunteered another girl. "Remember that time a lot of fish died somewhere near here because of a sewage backup."

"But wouldn't the problem have to be something really big, so big that the whales couldn't handle it?" Jonathan mused.

Pence, who was unsure about what to say and didn't want to speculate wildly, since Miss Burdick thought he was the class expert, finally piped up. "I read that gray whales usually dive through oil spills. And large spills rarely go unnoticed . . ."

"Who knows why?" Mr. Arnold interrupted, challenging the class further. When no one spoke up, he explained that weather satellites detect oil spills and other environmental mishaps. "So we'd know if a big spill had taken place nearby. Keep thinking," he added encouragingly. "What have we been talking about all this week?"

"The weather!" everyone screamed at once.

Mr. Arnold covered his ears before replying. "Exactly. You needn't shout your answers in the future, however. My hearing is adequate, or it was until a few seconds ago."

"But does weather explain why the whales are apparently detouring around San Diego?" Jonathan asked.

"I thought we had great weather," someone said, without thinking.

Mr. Arnold raised his eyebrows. "Jonathan has a point. We'll be docking in a few minutes, so we won't be able to solve this mystery today. But I want you all to think about it over the weekend. Do some research at the library. Don't be afraid to pursue any possibility. I've given you one—unusual weather—which is not a foolproof theory. Come up with at least one likely explanation and be able to document it scientifically."

The reporter was the first one off the boat.

Once ashore, Laura got permission to go directly home with Pence, and caught up with him.

"What a day," Pence murmured.

"And what a report you gave," Mr. Arnold complimented him, appearing as always when Pence least expected him.

"Thanks, Mr. Arnold," Pence replied, then added, "I thought you held a terrific science class today."

"There's nothing like an enigma, a puzzle to get the brain waves moving. I can't wait to get to a library," Mr. Arnold acknowledged, as he made a dash for the waiting bus.

Laura watched the reporter walk over and put a coin into the pay phone. He then began reading from a notebook to the person on the other end of the line.

7
OATH OF SILENCE

"What's the hurry?" Laura asked breathlessly, trying to keep up with Pence.

"I want to call my dad about something," he explained as they ran toward his house.

"What do you mean 'something'? Why don't you just say 'the missing whales'?"

"Remember what Mr. Arnold said, 'Don't jump to conclusions.' We don't know they're missing."

"I didn't think you paid much attention to what Mr. Arnold thought," Laura teased him.

Pence cleared his throat, thinking of the compliment Mr. Arnold had given him on his report. "Well, he's not all that bad. I know how he feels about wanting to do more research," Pence acknowledged, slowing his pace. "I want to get more facts. And I want to tell my dad about that reporter.

"Do you think he should be allowed to write a story about missing whales?" Pence demanded.

"You can't stop a reporter from writing a story he thinks is important."

Pence knew she was right, but he was edgy and upset about the whales. "I bet my dad will have an answer, or at least know how to find one. He's not just a penguin expert," he added proudly.

As they burst into the kitchen, he shouted "*Hola!*" to Carmen, told her Laura was here to help, and raced to the telephone.

"How did your talk go? How was the trip?" his father asked when Pence reached him at work.

"There weren't any whales. Both Miss Burdick and my science teacher think there's something wrong."

"Hold on, son. I've got another call."

While he waited for his father, Pence listened to Carmen and Laura, chattering in the kitchen.

"Lowra, you a big help to me," Carmen said warmly. "I wish we have more girls in this house. Even the *tortugas* are boys."

Laura laughed, then assured her that "Pence was working on that very problem."

"This teacher is nice?" Carmen asked hopefully.

Mr. Thompson came back on the line so Pence didn't catch Laura's response.

"That was Dr. Blair. I'm wanted at an urgent meeting. I'll be home as soon as I can."

"But, Dad," Pence protested.

"We'll talk about the whales tonight," his father said firmly.

Mr. Thompson still wasn't home when Miss Burdick arrived at seven o'clock sharp. Laura opened the door and explained that Pence was on a "reptile hunt" and would be down soon.

After discovering the errant Max under a dresser, Pence returned him to Turtle Park, where the ever-patient Mortimer was waiting. He ran down the stairs and apologized to Miss Burdick for not greeting her himself and then apologized for his father's lateness.

Brushing aside his concern, she calmly remarked, "What a wonderful home you have! It makes me realize how much I miss living close to the water. I bet it's lovely here at Christmas," she added.

Pence nodded, but silently thought, "Some Christmases are better than others."

"Maybe you should consider moving," Laura suggested boldly.

Pence stared at his friend. What is she up to? he wondered.

"As a matter of fact, I plan to spend part of the vacation looking for a new place. My apartment doesn't allow pets, and I'm getting a dog soon. My parents' black lab recently had a litter. When I went home at Thanksgiving, I picked one out. The pups will be ready to leave their mother in a few weeks. I'm so excited," she said, sounding like a kid.

"Are all the other pups spoken for?" Pence asked.

"I think there's one male left. Are you interested?"

"Well, I am, but it will take a lot to convince my dad," he admitted. "Maybe you can help." While his teacher shot him a puzzled look, he quickly changed his plan, renaming it A – B – D.

"Do you have any other plans for Christmas, Miss Burdick?" Laura asked cagily.

"Laura!" Pence protested.

Miss Burdick laughed. "It's all right, Pence. I never mind answering Laura's questions." She raised her eyebrows slightly, and added, "Although this time I don't know what she has in mind.

"If you're really interested, I had planned to go back East and stay with my parents in Connecticut. But my brother, David, is coming here instead. Frankly, I'm just as happy to stay here where it's warm."

Pence and Laura both made mental notes.

"I bet Pence would love to take you and your brother on one of his special behind-the-scenes tours of Sea World," Laura said, nudging Pence.

He nodded, wondering how, short of gagging her, he could prevent Laura from asking any more personal questions. She must have read his mind, because she excused herself, saying she had to check on dinner.

As Laura had guessed she would, Miss Burdick asked if she could see Pence's famous fish collection. She seemed to like everything in Pence's room and she listened to him carefully. He couldn't remember anyone, except his mother and father, of course, ever having shown as much interest in him. For a short time, he forgot about the missing whales.

Just as Pence began to relax, Miss Burdick asked, "Don't you have a picture of your mother anywhere?"

Of course he did. Hundreds of them in albums along with the framed picture he had hidden away that morning. Pence felt bad about it now. He brought out a whole stack of albums from a cabinet, even the ones that contained his baby pictures.

For several minutes they pored over the pictures. Pence paused every so often to explain where a particular one was taken. They laughed over many of them.

"She's lovely," said Miss Burdick warmly.

"My mother died of a blood disease. Her name was Sarah," he said softly.

"I think she would have been very proud of you."

He blushed. It seemed the perfect moment to

ask her if she could stay with him while his father was in the Antarctic. She'd say yes, he was sure. And she could keep her puppy at his house for those few weeks. But what if she said no?

"Anybody home?" his father called from the living room.

Pence let out a sigh of relief. Miss Burdick followed him downstairs, where Mr. Thompson shook her hand and said, "Hi. I'm Matt Thompson. We met at Back to School Night. Did you meet the turtles?"

"Not only the turtles, but also the fish," she answered cheerfully.

"Forgive me—both of you—for being late."

Pence was dying to ask his father what had kept him so long. What else could an *urgent* meeting have been about but the whales? Yet why would his father have been involved in that? Laura announced that dinner was "more than ready," so his questions would just have to wait.

After what seemed like hours of unimportant talk, Pence could contain himself no longer. "Dad, don't you want to hear about our trip?" he asked anxiously.

"I'm all ears."

Pence, Laura, and Miss Burdick all started talking at once.

"Hold it!" his father said, laughing. "Why doesn't *one* of you tell me what happened."

"Laura would love to," Miss Burdick offered.

When she had finished, Pence's father said, "If you'll all take an oath of silence, I'll tell you what I've learned about the whales in the last few hours."

The three of them quickly agreed.

"I didn't want to spoil your field trip, but we were informed of the irregularity two days ago. That's when the whales were first missed. Apparently, they were on course, on their normal migration route, until two days ago."

"They left the arctic region on schedule and were sighted at all the usual points along the coast. A large pod was seen about forty-five miles north of here late Tuesday. But, as you now know, they haven't made it here. Thousands more are on their way, and we're worried about them, too. No one is willing to say officially that the whales are missing, but it's certain that something unusual has occurred."

"Why hasn't there been anything in the news?" Pence and Laura both broke in at once.

"Actually, there was something on the local TV news tonight that might be related," Miss Burdick said. "The mayor's office announced that the beaches had been temporarily closed to swimmers and surfers, and no fishing was permitted until further notice."

Mr. Thompson nodded. "The Marine Fisheries

Service feels strongly that it's in everyone's best interest to stay out of the water, and, what's more, not take marine life out of it until they've had a chance to test for pollutants or chemicals. They've asked us to help."

"But why wasn't there any mention of the whales on the news report?" Miss Burdick inquired.

"The press isn't aware there *is* any problem with the whales," Mr. Thompson answered quietly.

"I wouldn't be too sure," Laura offered. "There was a reporter from the *Sentinel* on our trip today."

Mr. Thompson excused himself and went to make a phone call.

When he returned, Pence spoke up: "One of the kids in our class said they're drilling for oil in the breeding lagoons, Dad. Do you think the whales could be heading for some new area because of that?"

"It's possible, but I doubt it. Most of us at Sea World believe the whales are simply swimming farther offshore to avoid something in our waters. Two of our researchers are up at Oceanside right now. That's the point at which the whales were last seen."

"What about the lagoons? Isn't it possible some of the whales have arrived there already?" Miss Burdick asked.

"Yes. And that brings me to my next news." His father looked directly at Pence. "We've been asked to fly some of our staff down to Scammon's Lagoon tomorrow morning. Marine Fisheries wants us to count the number of whales, if any, that have arrived, and check their condition."

"It really is a crisis then," Miss Burdick said, thinking aloud.

Mr. Thompson nodded. "This isn't my area of expertise, but two of our top cetologists are out of the country, and Dr. Blair, our senior man, asked me to go along."

"That's great, Dad. Aren't you excited?" Pence asked, his voice full of admiration.

"Yes. I'd love to be able to help solve this mystery. If something is wrong, we all want to put an end to the problem fast."

Getting up from the table, Laura joked that it was time for the junior scientists to put an end to the dish-washing, fast.

Neither adult protested vigorously.

When the children were out of earshot, Miss Burdick said to Mr. Thompson, "Pence is a wonderful boy. I'm sure you know that. But he's been acting somewhat forlorn this week. Is Christmas a hard time for him?"

Mr. Thompson didn't know where to begin. The words just seemed to rush out all at once. "I'd thought of calling you. Is it all right if I call you Nancy?" he asked cautiously.

"My friends call me Rick," she answered matter-of-factly.

"What are they saying?" Pence whispered to Laura in the kitchen. She had her ear to the door.

"She just told him her nickname is 'Rick,'" Laura reported.

"It suits her better than 'Nancy,' don't you think?" he mused.

"Your Dad must think so. He's calling her 'Rick' now." She grinned at him.

"Well, Rick, I have to make a field trip to the Antarctic. I'll be gone for the entire Christmas vacation, plus another week," he explained. "Since we never know how severe the weather will be, our schedule is rarely certain."

"Who will Pence stay with?" she asked.

"Either he'll stay with our neighbors, the Lewises, as he usually does when I'm out of town overnight, or, I don't know." He shook his head. "Pence says he'd rather stay here with a housekeeper. Now, on top of that, I've also got to arrange for him to stay somewhere while I'm down at the lagoon, because the Lewises are away.

"I don't know why I'm burdening you with this,

Rick," he apologized. "Pence was so excited you could come for dinner, and all we've talked about so far are missing whales and my problems."

"I've had a very nice time, and I'm extremely fond of Pence," she assured him. "I don't mean to intrude, but if I can help in any way, feel free to ask."

Later, when he was walking her to her car, she asked tentatively, "Do you think Pence would want to stay with me over Christmas?"

He was momentarily speechless. "I *know* he would," he finally said. "He's a big fan of yours, Rick. But I couldn't ask that big a favor."

"Think about it, Matt. My vacation schedule is pretty open. I wish I could offer to do it now, but I'm off to a teacher conference, until Sunday afternoon."

"I think I'm going to tell Dr. Blair I couldn't find anyone to take Pence on such short notice, and ask if he can go with me. It's a safe trip, and we may need another hand down there," he mused.

"Is it all right if I call you when I, I mean *we*, get back?" he asked hopefully.

"I hope you will," she said, blushing. "I mean, um, that I'll be interested to hear about the whales."

8
EMERGENCY IN THE LAGOON

Laura was up earlier than usual the next morning. She immediately went outside to pick up the newspaper. There was nothing about whales on the front page, although the mayor's announcement prohibiting swimming and fishing was the lead story. She flipped through until she found an article headlined "Having a Whale of a Time." It was about her class's field trip, and the byline read, "By Ned Potter."

She read: "'Although the fifth graders did not see any whales, they were not disappointed. Their teachers managed to make the field trip interesting by asking the students to think of reasons the migrating gray whales had not yet appeared off our coast. . . .'"

Something was wrong for sure, Laura told herself as she carefully folded the paper back up and walked back indoors.

Why hadn't Mr. Potter written a front-page story on the missing whales? she asked herself as she poured Cheerios into a bowl. A good reporter would surely have seen that that was the real story.

On the drive to the airport, his father gave Pence some final instructions: "Be helpful without getting in the way. Remember, this is a crisis."

Pence nodded. He was too excited to speak.

Fog enveloped the airfield, but the pilot, Duke Mitchell, informed them they would take off shortly anyway. While his father talked with Dr. Blair and the two cetologists who would be flying down to the lagoon with them, Pence regarded the small, two-engine jet plane warily. He had never flown on anything but a big, commercial jet before.

As the pilots loaded the camera equipment, sleeping bags, and other supplies into the rear cargo compartment, Pence took his father aside and asked, "Can this small plane fly in so much fog?"

"This Lear 35A jet has flown some pretty precious cargo before, including penguin eggs all the way from Peru," his father assured him.

The pilots invited Pence to sit right behind the cockpit once they were in flight.

"How long will the flight be?" Pence asked, trying to take his mind off his worries.

"It's less than 400 miles. We should land in under an hour," the copilot told him.

"What does it feel like to fly a plane?"

"It isn't much different from driving a car," Duke Mitchell explained, "except for strong headwinds and electrical storms and being thousands of feet above the ground."

Pence peered out the window. There seemed to be no storms in sight. "Is it usually clear at Scammon's Lagoon?" he asked.

The pilot and copilot chuckled and exchanged glances. "No. We've found all kinds of weather there. On our last trip down, the airfield was unexpectedly closed." They didn't say that on that trip they had made a controlled crash landing in the desert.

Today the landing was smooth and skillfully executed. Their plane was met by a Mexican government official, who handed Dr. Blair several papers to sign. Scammon's Lagoon had been declared a private marine preserve in 1972, and official permission was needed to enter the area.

Two jeeps were waiting for them. The drive, on unpaved roads, across miles of desert and through the salt flats that surrounded part of the lagoon was a lot rougher than the plane ride, Pence thought, and took almost as long.

"We'll have to hike the rest of the way," Dr. Blair explained as the jeeps pulled off the road. "Bring

an inflatable boat, will you, Matt? I'll take the re-
cording instruments. Pence, carry the food baskets."

They rushed to the lagoon, propelled forward
by the need to know if the whales had arrived. Even
for those scientists who had been there many times,
the first glimpse of the lagoon was always exciting.
Tiny islands, inhabited only by crabs and other small
sand creatures, dotted the landscape. Sand dunes
cropped up here and there. The lagoon measured
from twenty feet deep in the middle to five feet deep
at the edges. Schools of fish were pursued by
bottlenose dolphins, which, once they had had
their fill, swam close to shore to greet the human
visitors. A few salt barges were moving along the
thirty-mile stretch of salt water.

"I understand now why the whales travel 6,000
miles to get here!" Pence exclaimed an hour later,
when they had all regrouped.

One of the cetologists, Dr. Helen Winston,
laughed and said, "Right now, there are probably
more dolphins than whales here, but close to 2,000
grays winter in this particular lagoon. I saw one
new calf out there. It can't be more than a day old.
I saw the mother's placenta floating nearby."

After allowing themselves ten minutes for lunch,
the scientists inflated the two seventeen-foot mo-
torized boats and headed for the entrance to the

lagoon. They watched with awe as dolphins and whales waited in turn to ride the Pacific tide into the calmer water.

"You can see why sailors stayed away from here. The entryway is treacherous," his father remarked to Pence. "You can also see why it took so long for anyone to discover the lagoon."

Not realizing anyone else was listening, Pence asked why a breeding lagoon was named for a whaler. It didn't seem right.

Dr. Blair had a ready answer. "In an odd way, we owe a lot to Charles Scammon. He was indeed a whaler—more than a hundred years ago—but he was also one of the first to realize that whales faced extinction if the slaughtering continued at such a high rate.

"It's easy for us to have perfect hindsight, Pence," he explained, "but we have to remember that whale meat and whale oil served important human needs back then. The invention of electricity probably saved more whales than anything else."

"I think the main thing to consider," Dr. Joshua Persky broke in, "is that many species are now protected. The California gray whale has been for over forty years and is thriving."

"All right, everyone. That concludes our lesson for today. We've got work to do!" Dr. Blair announced, then excused himself and went off to radio the pilots, telling them that they would make camp by the lagoon that night and should be back at the airfield by lunchtime, if all went well.

Pence followed Dr. Winston around for most of the afternoon. She was in charge of photographing the whales to document their physical condition and movements. He watched her closely and tried to take the same pictures she did.

"On my first trip to one of these breeding lagoons, I guess I got too close to a newborn calf. Its mother slammed against the side of the boat and sent me and my equipment flying," Dr. Winston told him.

"Are they often dangerous like that?"

"No. They're very gentle animals, unless provoked."

Pence spotted the others racing across the lagoon. "Where do you think they're going?"

"Quick, Pence, get back in the boat. They'll need our help," she instructed.

"What do you mean?"

"Look through my binoculars. There's a beached calf on one of the sand bars!"

It was going to be difficult to get the calf back in the water. It was close to sixteen feet long. The mother whale couldn't get close enough to help, and she was three times its size. The baby seemed frightened and confused.

Dr. Blair was shouting orders when Pence and

Dr. Winston got there. "Don't strain yourselves. This baby must weigh close to a ton."

"Doc," he yelled at Dr. Winston, "keep the calf wet somehow." Pence knew that if its skin dried out, it would die.

While the three men tried to push, roll, or drag the unwieldy calf back into the lagoon, Pence helped Dr. Winston. With only their hands and her shade hat for tools, they worked to keep the calf moist. No barnacles yet clung to the dark, unmottled skin, which Dr. Winston patted gently when she wasn't dousing it with water.

Stopping to catch his breath, Pence's father said, "There must be a better way. What about the tide? When it comes in, won't it do the job for us?"

"We can't chance it," Dr. Blair answered. "I've seen high tides in this lagoon. Sometimes the waves are huge. Stranded calves can drown if caught in that kind of incoming tide."

No one was willing to admit defeat, however.

"If we could only hoist it up somehow," said Dr. Winston, thinking aloud.

"If we could borrow some shovels from those workers over on the sand flats, we could dig around the calf enough to at least loosen the sand," offered Dr. Persky.

"I've got an idea," yelled Pence's father as he ran to one of the inflatable boats.

Within minutes he was back, followed by a sand

barge filled with Mexican workers and long coils of rope.

After they tied the whale securely with five long, sturdy ropes, they secured the end of each to a hook welded to the side of the barge.

Meanwhile, the mother whale splashed wildly against the barge. There was no way to calm her down. They hoped she wouldn't upset the barge— their only chance.

The captain started the engine, but it wouldn't turn over.

"Don't flood it!" Dr. Blair shouted to him in Spanish. "There are fifteen-foot waves out there. We've got to get this calf off the sand bar before the tide comes in."

Miraculously, they did. The barge moved slowly at first, creaking from the weight. But steadily it pulled the calf to safety.

The mother, still thinking her baby was in danger, breached furiously and rammed the barge a few more times, knocking one of the workers into the water. The man screamed and thrashed about in the lagoon until he was pulled back up on board, holding onto the outstretched hands for dear life.

The calf was quickly untied. Free at last, it swam to its mother, who nudged it affectionately for several minutes. Drenched with sweat and salt water, the humans watched as the mother and calf swam to a more secluded and less dangerous part of the lagoon.

That night, Drs. Blair and Winston posted themselves at the lagoon entrance. Dr. Persky and Dr. Thompson monitored the behavior of two newly arrived pregnant whales.

When his father wasn't busy for a moment, Pence asked, "What would have happened to the calf if we hadn't been here, Dad?"

"I think it's fair to say we saved a life today," his father answered.

Pence crawled into his sleeping bag well past midnight and listened to the haunting cry of coyotes in the distance. He wished he weren't so tired; he wished he knew more about whales and could have helped more.

His father stuck his head in. "You were right about Miss Burdick. She must be a terrific teacher. Did you know she was from back East, too?"

Pence nodded.

"If we solve this crisis, I leave for the Antarctic a week from today, son. I'd like Miss Burdick to be the one who stays with you. There's something I haven't told you. She offered to! Did you hear me, Pence?"

No, he hadn't. Mr. Thompson kissed his sleeping son on the forehead and went back to help Dr. Persky. Both whales gave birth before dawn.

9
STRANGE
HAPPENINGS

"I'm going to head over to Sea World, Pence. We've got a meeting at six," his father said, sticking his head in the room. Pence was lying on his bed scanning the Sunday paper for news about the whales. He looked at the clock on his desk.

"But it's only three," he observed. "We've only been home a little while."

"Don't you have homework?"

"I've done all of it except for the science paper. I was hoping you'd have a chance to tell me what you all discussed on the flight back. Can't you stay a little longer, Dad?" Pence asked hopefully.

"Sure I can." His father pushed aside some papers and books and sat down next to Pence.

"We agreed there was nothing unusual about the whales' behavior or appearance at the lagoon. That was Dr. Blair on the phone a few minutes ago. He just got word from one of our research teams that hundreds of whales have been sighted swimming about fifteen miles west of here, then coming back to the coastline farther south. They are making a big detour."

"So the problem is *here*, isn't it, Dad?"

His father nodded. "No question about it now. But we have more work ahead of us. Dr. Winston is checking into the possibility of some kind of unreported spill. Dr. Persky is looking into the amount of boat traffic and whether any underwater research is being conducted near here that might alter the marine life ecosystem."

"What's your job?" Pence asked.

"Migratory patterns and why they sometimes vary. After all, I'm the bird man." He grinned. "I have a hunch, but I need to do some fact-checking at my office," he explained, looking at his watch.

"I guess you better get going, then," Pence remarked.

"I may be late tonight. Do you think you can make yourself a sandwich or something for dinner?"

"Sure, Dad. And thanks. I've got enough information to finish my paper on whales now."

Dr. Thompson uncharacteristically raced out the door. Pence knew his father was excited about something but didn't believe it was merely the inexplicable wanderings of the whales.

Later, he went down to the kitchen to see about food. As he searched the refrigerator, an unexpected noise made him turn around. He could have sworn the electric can opener had just gone on, taken half a turn, and then gone off.

Nothing unusual occurred in the next few minutes, but Pence decided to write his report downstairs, just to keep an eye on things. He didn't mind staying home alone for a few hours; long ago he had gotten used to the unexplained noises their house made. Today, though, he felt uneasy. Unsettling thoughts about poltergeists and alien invaders interfered with his concentration. He dialed Sam's number, but no one answered. Now and then he peered over his shoulder at the can opener. When the sound of his own heartbeat startled him, he dropped his pen and raced over to Laura's.

She must have seen him coming, since she opened the front door before he had a chance to ring the bell. Just seeing her inquisitive expression, her mouth already forming a question, calmed his shaky nerves.

"So were there any whales or not? I can't stand the suspense," Laura pleaded. "If you learned something important about the whales, tell me!"

"A few were at the lagoon, and they were fine."

"So it's still a mystery?" Laura broke in.

Pence nodded. "Something in or around San

Diego is frightening them, or at least causing them to avoid our coast," he reported.

Laura seemed a little disappointed. She'd been hoping for more dramatic news, maybe even that Pence had helped solve the crisis.

Mrs. Kiefer invited him to stay for Sunday supper, and he had the opportunity to describe his trip in great detail to Laura and her family. They were all ears and, afterward, full of questions. Laura was the youngest of four children, but Pence noticed that she led the conversation at home as well as in school.

It was close to nine o'clock when Mr. Kiefer drove Pence home. Pence noticed that the garage door was open. He was sure his father had closed it before he left, but he didn't say anything. Mr. Kiefer walked him to the door and stayed long enough to make sure Pence was safely locked in.

Pence swallowed hard a few times, but went directly to the garage to make sure nothing was missing. Everything seemed okay. But when the garage door suddenly began to close of its own accord—or because of some invisible force—he had to cover his mouth to stop from screaming.

He told himself to be calm, took a few deep breaths, and walked into the house. He tried to convince himself that there was some reasonable explanation. Of course there was! Carmen had told him about the garage door the other day, but he hadn't remembered to tell his father. Laughing, he sat down at the kitchen table to finish his report. Just then his eyes confirmed what his ears had told him before: the electric can opener was in motion, its gears grinding. And with no can to open and no one there turning it on and then off!

Pence jumped out of his chair and turned on the TV in the family room. He flipped the dial until he found a news program about to deliver a weekend wrap-up. Eight minutes of local news produced nothing about an alien attack that caused whales to veer off a path they'd been traveling for hundreds of years and garage doors and can openers to work by themselves.

When Mr. Thompson came home much later, he found Pence asleep, still dressed and with his homework spread out over the floor. He leaned over to kiss him on the forehead, and Pence woke with a start.

"What's the matter? You look like you've seen a ghost," his father said, looking worried.

"I had kind of a scare while you were gone," Pence said, sitting up and rubbing his eyes. "The garage door closed by itself and the can opener turned itself on and off."

"Is that all?" His father seemed relieved. "That used to happen a lot when we first moved here. It has something to do with our being so close to the flight path of Lindbergh Field."

"But what if there's some connection between the whales and our garage door?"

His father raised his eyebrows. "Pence, be serious."

"I am, Dad. What makes the whales follow a certain route year after year?" he asked urgently.

"You heard Dr. Persky at the lagoon. We don't know for sure, but we know fin whales follow a north-south magnetic field the way humans follow a highway," he answered, beginning to follow Pence's line of thought.

He stood up and paced back and forth, pushing his temples as if to stimulate his brain waves.

"A number of things can interfere with a magnetic field," he said, thinking aloud. "And most whale strandings occur where the lines of the magnetic field are weak." Turning to Pence he added, "Homing pigeons and bees face similar problems in the air."

"What about that mild earthquake we had ten days ago? Wouldn't that have shaken things up? Come to think of it," he continued excitedly, "it was centered close to where the whales were first missed!"

His father shook his head. "We've already discussed the earthquake possibility with several geophysicists. They haven't noticed any disturbance of marine life as a result. Sorry. You get an A for effort, though." His father smiled at him.

Pence wasn't discouraged. "How about this, then. An enemy nation wants to monitor our defense system. They've planted some kind of surveillance device outside the harbor. All the beeping disturbs the whales, and they swim around it."

"All that beeping would have disturbed the Navy, too. They're always on top of what's going on in and around our waters," his father reminded him.

Looking at his father squarely, Pence said, "You still have friends in the Navy, Dad. Why don't you ask one of them to dig around? It's worth a try."

"It's late, Pence. Put your pajamas on and get some sleep."

"Okay, but at least tell me what happened tonight."

"We ruled out pollution and unusual currents. But the newspapers have got wind of the problem and are pressuring us for information. A Mr. Potter from the *Sentinel* told us he's going to publish a story about 'missing whales' if we hold back any news! And the mayor's worried that tourists will be scared away, too." He groaned.

Pence giggled. "Maybe it's Jaws V!"

His father covered his ears, gave Pence another kiss, and went downstairs. He quietly closed the family-room door and dialed the number of an old friend. "I'm sorry to disturb you at this hour, Frank. This is Matt Thompson. I need to talk to you about some missing whales. . . ."

When Pence woke the next morning, his father had already left for work. There was a note on the refrigerator.

I'm proud of you. I'll call you after school. Keep what you and I discussed last night to yourself. I can't say more now.   *Love, Dad*

The morning paper was spread out on the counter. His father had circled a short article: *"Where Were You When the Garage Doors Moved?"* The article began, *"If your garage doors recently opened and closed all by themselves, you're not alone. The San Diego Police Department received close to 100 calls this past week from panicky citizens who claimed their electrically controlled garage doors inexplicably moved of their own accord. One woman swore she had seen a ghost push the button of her neighbor's garage. Three people were hospitalized, suffering shock, but all were released.*

"Police Chief Robert Daniels commented, 'We get

a lot of prank calls around Halloween and at first we thought this was just another round of the same, but several members of the force have stated that they, too, witnessed such occurrences when responding to 911 calls.'"

10
PERSISTENCE

Mr. Arnold was engrossed in conversation with Miss Burdick outside her classroom when Pence arrived. He was relieved to hear they'd only been discussing the whales.

"Miss Burdick told me you went to Scammon's Lagoon, Pence," Mr. Arnold said in greeting. "I can't wait to hear all about it, and what Sea World has found out. I wish we could move our class up to first period today."

Pence smiled at him. "I'm kind of impatient myself."

When Jonathan sauntered in, Pence took him aside. "I forgot to tell you one vital piece of information over the phone last night. I took three rolls of film at the lagoon. If Miss Burdick will excuse you from recess, you could develop them in the lab."

"And if she won't, I could say I felt sick, and

instead of going to the nurse's station I could dart into the lab," Jonathan plotted.

"Great," Pence replied, shaking his head. "And then you'd be sent to Mr. Moore's office for the zillionth time!"

"I see your point," Jonathan said, slightly disgusted with himself. "Well, you have to be there when I ask her."

Miss Burdick hesitated at first, but seeing the eager looks on their faces, she agreed to let Jonathan use the lab during the morning recess period.

Instead of heading for the teacher's room at recess, Miss Burdick walked out to the playground. As Pence was about to shoot baskets with the other boys, she called to him.

"Let's take a walk," she suggested.

"I've had a long talk with your father," she began. "I know about his trip to the Antarctic and about your wanting to stay in your house while he's away."

Pence gulped.

Miss Burdick looked straight at him and continued uncertainly. "I volunteered to stay with you. Would that be all right?"

"Sure," Pence answered immediately, trying to hide his pleasure. "We have lots of room."

Miss Burdick laughed. She looked as if she was going to hug him but held back. "We'll talk about it later this week. I'm happy you said yes. It will take a big load off your father's mind."

That makes two of us, Pence thought to himself. He didn't know how he would make it through the rest of the school day. He was overwhelmed by the news and, suddenly, looking forward to Christmas vacation.

After recess, Jonathan burst into the classroom dangling the still-wet photographs from clips. Laura was right behind him with more. Miss Burdick told them to lay the pictures out on the display table, which she quickly cleared.

Everyone got up and pushed to the front of the room to have a look. There were good close-ups of a pod entering the lagoon, and of the newborn calf following its mother. There was even one of a Commerson's dolphin.

Jonathan had a dazed look on his face. "I'm in love," he sighed dreamily. "With Scammon's Lagoon, that is. Couldn't we plan a trip to one of the breeding lagoons, Miss Burdick? Maybe even this winter."

Everyone shouted at once. "Great idea!" "Way to go, Glazer." "Maybe we could camp out there!"

Miss Burdick finally quieted them all down, and beaming at Jonathan observed, "We have just enough time to compose a letter to the Mexican government before lunch."

Meanwhile, over at Sea World, behind closed doors, Dr. Blair wrote a new theory on the crowded blackboard, then erased two others they had determined were off target. He listened to more reports from staff researchers on the status of the whales. After the researchers left, another group came in, headed by Alexander Thornhill, Sea World's chairman. Two hours later, with strategies planned, Mr. Thornhill shook hands with everyone and congratulated them on their efforts.

"I'm sorry, we won't have time to read all of your papers today," Mr. Arnold said to the class. "Let's get to the heart of the matter. One at a time, briefly tell me your ideas."

He listed on the board the various suggestions. When it was Pence's turn, he still hadn't figured out what he was going to say. Since his father had asked him to keep their talk to himself, he fudged.

"Whales are highly intelligent. Even though they are coastal animals, they'll swim off course by as much as twenty-five miles to avoid something they think is dangerous."

A classmate interrupted impatiently. "What do the people at Sea World think?"

"What about the news story on possible hazardous pollutants in the water that could endanger marine life?" asked someone else.

"Well, they're still testing the water for unusual substances and checking to see if the number of boats is way above other years," he replied, hoping that would satisfy them.

Laura piped up. "Did anyone see the article in this morning's paper about humpback whales moving farther off the Atlantic shore to avoid the tourist boats there?"

Mr. Arnold nodded but pressed on. "I want to narrow the possibilities," he said. "How many of you think a pollutant of some kind is causing the whales to swim around San Diego?" Five students raised their hands. "How many of you think the whales are simply avoiding overcrowded waters?" Eleven students raised their hands, Laura among them. "Who thinks nothing is seriously wrong, that it's just an irregularity?" The rest of the class, except for Pence and Jonathan, raised their hands.

Mr. Arnold eyed them both. "Do either of you have another explanation?"

"All weekend I kept thinking about the earthquake we had right after Thanksgiving," Jonathan answered. "It was centered in Oceanside, near the point where the whales were last seen. Right, Spenser?"

Pence couldn't believe his ears. What could he do but nod? If Jonathan thought there might be some connection between the earthquake and the whales' movements, Pence was convinced he himself was on the right track. He couldn't, however, bring himself to suggest the garage-door incident as somehow related.

A knock on the door saved him. The school secretary handed a note to Miss Burdick who then whispered something to Pence. He walked to his desk, collected his books, and left without a word.

"It seems Pence is wanted at Sea World," she revealed to the class.

Mr. Arnold was not to be deterred. "What do we know about earthquakes, and how they affect marine life?" he asked excitedly.

No one raised his hand right away. Like their classmates, neither Laura nor Jonathan felt like sitting through the rest of science class with Pence on his way to Sea World. But Mr. Arnold drew them back, encouraging them to solve the mystery. He felt they were getting close.

11
FRONT-PAGE NEWS, FINALLY

His father was waiting for Pence outside the west gate of the park. He flashed his employee pass at the guard, and they went in.

"What's happened, Dad?"

"All I can tell you is there's to be a press conference about the whales. Hurry! We were supposed to be in Mr. Thornhill's office five minutes ago."

Just the thought of Sea World's six-foot-four, 220-pound chairman sent panic through his system. In his experience, Mr. Thornhill didn't speak, he growled.

The administration building was swarming with people. Many of them had cameras, and most wore press badges. Mr. Thompson grabbed Pence by the hand and together they pushed their way through the boisterous crowd.

Pence got separated from his father and was

cornered by a reporter, who said, "What are you doing here, kid?" He saw the reporter from the boat trip out of the corner of his eye. Then suddenly microphones were thrust at him from all sides, notebooks were flipped open, and tape recorders switched on. Cameras flashed, momentarily blinding him.

"That will be enough, ladies and gentlemen of the press!" boomed a voice. "I need to speak to this young man in my office for a moment."

Mr. Thornhill motioned Pence to follow him, as the crowd parted to let Pence through. Soon they were in the chairman's office, safe from the reporters.

Pence stared first at the office which was grander than he had imagined, then at dozens of faces smiling at *him*.

"Have a seat, Pence." Mr. Thornhill gestured from behind an enormous mahogany desk. "We've been waiting for you. I'm on a tight schedule. Like the gray whales," he added with a smile. "We learned why the whales have been avoiding this area, and all of us here feel it was due to your persistence that we solved the mystery so quickly—and painlessly, I might add," Mr. Thornhill said.

"First, let me introduce some of the people here you don't know who want to thank you in person. Admiral Franklin Parker, Dr. Keith Henderson . . ."

Pence shook hands with everyone, but still couldn't understand why all these important people seemed glad to meet him.

"Admiral, why don't you explain," Mr. Thornhill suggested.

"What I have to say must go no farther than this room," Admiral Parker began. "For the present at least, it is classified information. I received a telephone call from Matt Thompson late last night. Pence, your father was an officer in my command years ago, in case you didn't know." The admiral beamed at him, while Pence studied the two stars on his shoulder boards.

"He told me that the gray whales were avoiding the area and he wondered if the Navy had a clue as to why. He said his ten-year-old son thought the whales might be reacting to some magnetic change. Matt explained that if anything was disturbing the magnetic field, the Navy would be the first to know about it. Pence urged him to call us." Admiral Parker smiled. "I'm glad he did."

"A number of unfriendly nations have dispatched submarines to our waters in the past year. We felt security should be tightened." So, he told them, the Navy had, with the President's knowledge, been laying highly sensitive surveillance equipment just beyond the harbor.

"Pence, your father told me about the garage

door and the can opener." He chuckled. "A number of San Diegans had the same experience. Police Chief Daniels quickly called the Navy, before the press started writing stories about an alien invasion."

"But what about the whales?" Pence asked. "Will they stop coming here forever?"

"Not a chance," his father spoke up. "Admiral Parker says that soon the navy will install lower-frequency grids. Their undersea research and development center is working overtime to determine what frequencies the whales and other marine life will tolerate."

Pence let out a big sigh of relief. "You had me worried."

Everyone laughed. Pence blushed, but kept going. "Was the earthquake to blame in part?"

"We're still working on that question," the admiral replied.

Dr. Blair added, "One prominent geophysicist says the ocean is a very noisy environment anyway, and that earthquake tremors on the order of the one we recently experienced may have startled the whales, but nothing more. However, an expert at the National Earthquake Information Center, in Colorado, is convinced that earthquakes disturb magnetic fields, throwing them off by several degrees.

"After the big earthquake in Mexico City, inner

tidal sea life studies showed a permanent deformity of the earth's surface," he added.

"The reporters sound like they're getting pretty restless," observed Mr. Thornhill. "I think it's time we satisfied their curiosity."

As Pence reached the door, Mr. Thornhill put a hand on his shoulder to stop him.

"I hope you're not angry with me, sir," Pence said, feeling somewhat uncomfortable. "I don't want you to think I was prying into your or the government's business."

Mr. Thornhill dismissed the idea. "No, no. On the contrary, I owe you something. How would you like to accompany your father on a field trip to the Galápagos Islands next summer? I've asked him to study penguin life there."

"Oh Mr. Thornhill, I just can't believe it. And to think I thought you were, well, mean."

The chairman let out a thunderous laugh. "Believe it, Pence. Now I have to face those reporters. They're always misquoting me.

"I have a feeling you and I will make tomorrow's front page. I'm going to release our latest research into how marine animals respond to magnetic fields, pointing to the earthquake as a possible culprit. Then I'll explain that the ten-year-old son of one of our best scientists pointed us—and the whales—in the right direction." He winked at Pence.

12
AN EARLY CHRISTMAS

Mr. Thornhill was right. Headlines on front pages read: TEN-YEAR-OLD SOLVES MYSTERY OF MISSING WHALES and WHALE EXPERTS DIRECTED TO MAGNETIC FIELD SOLUTION BY YOUNG SPENSER THOMPSON.

After his picture appeared on the front page of all four local newspapers and even one national newspaper, and he and the whales were the opening feature on all the nightly news programs in San Diego, Pence became the subject of much gossip at school. Some of it was fantastic. Pence overheard one boy tell another, "That Thompson kid single-handedly caught a gray whale in Scammon's Lagoon!"

Jonathan told Pence, "I'm glad *you're* the center of attention for a change. Try to take it in stride, Spenser."

Pence tried, but quickly decided that anonymity was a lot better than celebrity. He was almost relieved when his father got permission to take him out of school two days early, so they could have time together before he left on his trip.

They spent hours trimming the nine-foot Douglas fir they bought at a tree farm out in the country, and ended up eating all the popcorn they had planned to string then hang along the outer branches.

Pence carefully hung five stockings from the mantel.

"Why so many?" his father wanted to know.

"One for you. One for Mom. One for me. One for Miss Burdick. And the last one is for the dog."

"What was that last word?"

Pence looked down at his feet when he answered. "Didn't I tell you about Miss Burdick's new dog? And there's one more in the litter without a home."

"You know you didn't, or you wouldn't be looking at the floor," his father scolded.

Changing his tone, he added, "I don't think I want to know about this until I come back. But, like any good scientist, I've already drawn several conclusions. Let me say that I won't be surprised to find a member of the canine family in residence when I return." His frown quickly turned into a smile.

"You're the best dad in the whole, entire world! I knew you wouldn't say no," Pence shouted merrily, grabbing his father and squeezing him affectionately. "Wait till I tell Miss Burdick!"

"I hope Carmen doesn't faint when you tell *her*. She's always saying it's unhealthy to live in a house where there are more pets than people."

"So let's add another person," Pence breezily suggested.

His father looked embarrassed and quickly switched to another subject. "Did Carmen tell you what she's planned for our early Christmas dinner tomorrow night? All our favorite things—turkey with her special sausage stuffing, cranberry biscuits, fresh coconut cake. She told me she wanted to fatten me up before I went off to what she called 'Terra Freezing.' " He laughed.

"All that food for just the two of us?" Pence asked nonchalantly.

"Well, you and Miss Burdick and her brother are having dinner at the Lewises Christmas Day. Of course, if you want to invite her to join us for *our* Christmas dinner, it's fine with me."

"Only if you want to, Dad," Pence said, feigning dispassion.

"You're right. We *should* invite her!"

They looked at one another and burst out laughing.

Laura rushed in on the afternoon school closed for vacation, with stories about Christmas parties and who had given what present to whom. She assured Pence that he hadn't missed out on much except candy, and she pulled a bag of it for him from her backpack.

She giggled, though, when describing their last science class. "We finished our discussion of the whales and their sensitivity to sound. Mr. Arnold had told us we'd talk about the sounds of Christmas today. But we didn't expect him to show up dressed as Santa and waving an enormous bell. His beard drooped, and the pillow fell out from under his shirt! He was so funny."

They both gulped with laughter.

"I'm sorry I wasn't there."

"I brought your dad something. Is he here?"

"He's upstairs packing. I'll go get him." Pence wondered if Laura had a present for him, too, but didn't see one. He had spent a lot of his savings buying her hair combs. It was Jonathan's idea. Pence had wanted to get her a pen set, but Jonathan assured him "you only give pen sets to teachers you despise."

"Laura's downstairs and has something for you. By the way, what did you get me for Christmas?" Pence asked his father who was having difficulty packing, judging from the piles of clothes strewn all over the room.

"It's one thing to have Christmas dinner three days early, but you'll just have to wait until Christmas, like everyone else, to open your presents," his father teased. "Of course," he continued, "you'll probably want to give me my presents tonight."

Pence shook his head. "Santa stops in the Antarctic. You'll have to wait, too. But, just in case, leave a little extra room in your suitcase. And no peeking!"

While Pence was upstairs, Laura put her present to him—a book about the Galápagos—under the tree.

Unwrapping the gift Laura handed him, Mr. Thompson said, "I'm glad someone around here is willing to bend the rules a little about present-giving." Underneath layers of colorful paper was a red diary.

"It's so handsome," he exclaimed, "and I really needed it, Laura. I'm always writing important things down on scraps of paper."

"Pence told me." Laura grinned at him.

"But what's this?" he asked, trying to read some writing inside the diary.

"Well, I hope you don't mind, Mr. Thompson. It's a list of questions I had about the Antarctic and the penguins' habitat that I hoped you'd have a chance to answer while you're there." She blushed.

"I'll do my best," he said, giving her a hug. "Laura, someday you're going to make someone a very good reporter!"

After Laura left, Pence helped his father finish packing. It wasn't long before Miss Burdick arrived, with a carload of her things. Pence helped her carry them to the guest room, and his father showed her where everything was.

Later that evening, full from Carmen's sumptuous feast, the three of them went for a walk. They sang Christmas carols while they strolled around Mission Bay, pretending the sand was snow.

Pence wandered off to look for crabs and unoccupied shells.

"I love it here," Miss Burdick said softly.

Mr. Thompson took her hand and covered it with his. "Pence and I love having you here with us."

They stood there gazing at each other without speaking until Pence returned, dangling a ghost crab. "Isn't he a beauty?" he asked the preoccupied grown-ups. "By the way, Dad, you never answered my question about whether or not crabs hear?"

Looking fondly at Miss Burdick his father replied, "You'll have to admit there have been an unusual number of distractions these last weeks. Maybe you two could find out the answer while I'm gone."

"I don't know if we'll have time. We have a lot of exciting things planned already." Pence smiled at his teacher.

"It looks like I won't be missed as much as I

thought," his father said, knowing that wouldn't be the case. "But try to remember what I've taught you, Pence."

"I'll always remember. Never stop looking for answers."

The night air had grown cold. The three of them ran home to continue their talk of important things.

Dear Pence,

It's freezing down here, but the penguins don't seem to mind.

I miss you. Tell Laura I got her card. I hope you and Rick are having fun. I can't wait to see you both

Love,
Dad

Pence Thompson
78 Crown Point Drive
San Diego, CA
92119

ANTARCTICA
JAN 3
U.S.P. ...
.44

Author Acknowledgments

I wish to thank the many dedicated scientists and staff members of Sea World, whose assistance was invaluable in the research and writing of this book, especially Dr. Lanny Cornell, David Butcher, Frank Todd, Frank Toohy, and Donald Hall. Dr. William Evans, former executive director of Sea World Research Institute/Hubbs Marine Research Center, now assistant administrator for fisheries, National Marine Fisheries, NOSS, generously shared his research experiences and lent me needed out-of-print books.

Willa Perlman and Rubin Pfeffer offered their intelligence, concern, and humor throughout.

I am indebted to my publisher William Jovanovich for his fervent red pencil and support. His brilliance and art of instruction continue to astound all those who are fortunate enough to work with him.